Dark Covenants

Edited by Kevin Wright

Table of Contents

Captives

By Russell Jones

JACOB ANSWERED THE PHONE ON THE FIRST RING, a cold pit in his stomach. He listened to the automated voice on the other end.

"Yes, I'll accept the charges."

A click. Then... "I'm going to fucking kill myself."

Jacob put his hand on the wall to steady himself, next to a rough wooden cross. "Samantha, we talked about that. It would be very bad if you did that. It would make the people who love you very upset."

A snort. "Nobody gives a shit. That's why I got shoved into this fucking hole and buried, so nobody would have to look at me."

"No, we sent you to the hospital so you could get better. So that people will be able to look after you all the time, take care of you the way we can't."

A sniffle. Silence. "I'm still going to die in here."

Captives

Jacob took a deep breath. A framed picture next to the phone showed a baby girl with curly blonde hair and shining eyes, smiling at the person taking the photo. A calendar behind it had a big red circle drawn around that day's date.

"Why do you think you're going to die?"

"The dreams."

"What do the dreams tell you?"

The phone suddenly crackled, as if it had been dropped and picked up again. The voice that answered was deeper and held far more conviction.

"THAT I'M GOING CRAWL OUT FROM UNDER HER SKIN AND TEAR HER HEART OUT."

"Samantha?" Jacob shouted into the phone, panic spreading through his gut. "Samantha, are you still there?"

The phone crackled again. Jacob thought he heard a growl.

"NOT FOR LONG."

* * * *

Jacob's secretary promised she'd take care of his appointments while he was out of the state. He'd still be able to use social media to check in on the 2,000 members who came to him for guidance, support, or prayer requests, but he could only serve his flock so well without face-to-face contact. It helped that the church employed a small army of lay leaders to back him up; they'd been more than happy in the past to step in when his "family troubles" had flared up.

His plane touched down before daybreak, and he was able to catch a nap on the cab ride out to the hospital's campus out in the country. He paid the driver extra, asking him to come back and pick him up at dusk. The older man seemed quite eager to get off the property, speeding away after taking Jacob's cash.

The imposing, crumbling building had been built almost a century before by an order of nuns. A private firm bought it after they fell on hard times and turned it into a place which specialized first and foremost in discretion rather than loving and tender care for all God's children.

Discretion was a trait Jacob valued as well, and very willing to pay for.

The orderlies at the front were different from his last visit, but efficient. He was quickly credentialed and escorted past the bustling common rooms full of docile, smocked patients and into a much quieter portion of the hospital. The doors were thicker, as were the orderlies, and there wasn't a single scrap of information anywhere which could identify who was in for treatment.

Captives

His chaperone keyed him through two sets of doors and into a small room with a metal table and two chairs. There was a door on the opposite side of the room but no windows or mirrors. Certainly no cameras.

Jacob set his bible down on the table and waited. He considered thumbing through its well-worn, highlighted pages to review a few pertinent passages, but the door across the room opened before he got the chance.

Two massive men squeezed through the door, supporting a waif-like girl between them. Her blonde hair was matted and stringy, frayed like the edges of a torn dress. They gingerly guided her onto the other metal chair then produced restraints which they used to bind her ankles, wrists, elbows and knees to it. The whole time her head lolled back, eyes glazed and unfocused on the world around.

The pair of orderlies finished then stood behind the chair and looked at Jacob expectantly.

"Leave," he said.

They exchanged glances then exited the way they came in. Jacob looked at the girl across from him and sighed. This was going to take some time.

* * * *

Hours passed. The girl's head lolled and occasionally murmured nonsense. Jacob sat in his chair, eyes closed and arms folded across his chest. There were no clocks to track the time, and he'd made sure to leave his phone, watch, and everything else besides his bible in the lobby. Noon came and passed with no change in either of their behavior and no disturbance from overly concerned orderlies bearing food or water.

Around the seventh hour, Jacob sighed. "I can do this all night as well, if necessary."

The lolling and murmuring stopped. The girl's head rolled forward, and she stared at the space between them.

"J ... Jay? Is that you?"

Jacob said nothing.

"Did I do something, Jay? I don't remember ... they gave me something..."

"God hates liars."

The girl stared at him in confusion. "What's happening, Jay? Did I do something wrong? Did I ... did I hurt someone again?"

Jacob kept his arms folded and eyes closed. "They're under strict orders not to give you any narcotics. You're faking it."

Captives

The girl strained at her bindings. "You prick," she spat, "lock me up just so you can come down here and yell at me, like some fucking high and mighty..."

"And stop using her voice," Jacob said. "There's really no need for that. Only a frightened, heathen coward would hide behind a little girl."

She stopped moving, letting her hair hang limply in front of her face. Jacob's skin prickled as the temperature dropped twenty degrees in a matter of seconds.

He opened his eyes.

Her breath was steaming in the frosty air, causing her sweat-streaked hair to shift and sway. He couldn't see her eyes, and that was just as well. He had a feeling they would not be the blazing blue he remembered from when she was just a toddler and ran screaming with joy through the tall grass on the farm.

She shifted in the chair, causing it to scrape harshly on the floor. It didn't sound like it was supporting the weight of a 90-pound girl. It sounded like it held something much ... heavier.

"YOU KNOW MUCH OF COWARDICE."

The voice was a harsh growl, all pus-soaked gravel ground between two pieces of rotten meat. A wave of smell accompanied it, like filth-covered sheets after a sick child's nightmare.

"What have I to fear?" Jacob asked. "The Lord is my shepherd; I shall not want."

The girl's bony shoulders shuddered, and her chest rocked as she loosed a wild cackle. Jacob had heard similar laughter during a nature documentary, when hyenas caught up to their prey and were just about to rip its legs off.

"BIG TALK FROM A MAN WITH SEVEN FIGURES IN THE BANK AND HIS OWN JET."

"Earthly riches mean nothing to me, for mine is the kingdom of Heaven."

"DOES THAT KINGDOM COME WITH HOT LITTLE BLONDES IN THE FRONT ROW OF THE CHURCH CHOIR?"

Jacob stayed silent. The girl grinned, and opened her mouth; the voice which came out was huskier, more seductive.

"NO, BROTHER JACOB, NOT WHILE MY HUSBAND'S IN AFGHANISTAN. I WOULDN'T WANT TO BETRAY HIS SACRIFICE."

Jacob said nothing.

The voice shifted again, becoming accusatory. *"THEN SUDDENLY HUBBY'S PATROL GOT REASSIGNED INTO AN AMBUSH. WHICH IS FUNNY,*

CONSIDERING HIS SQUAD LEADER'S GOING TO FILL IN FOR YOU IN THE PULPIT TOMORROW, ISN'T HE?"

"The Lord works in mysterious ways. His plans are not for all to know."

The girl's head cocked sideways. *"SO I'M PART OF THE PLAN, NOW? NOT SOME MISTAKE YOU SHIPPED OUT TO A CORNFIELD WHERE NOBODY WOULD EVER FIND ME?"*

The girl stretched forward as far as the restraints would allow. *"WAS IT HIS PLAN WHEN I DROVE AN ICE PICK INTO MY MOTHER'S FACE TWENTY-THREE TIMES? WHEN I CARVED YOUR NAME INTO HER CHEST AND DANCED IN THE ASHES OF HER BURNING HOUSE?"*

Jacob flinched. "That wasn't her. That was you. She was a lost lamb, and you tried to steal her away from the Lord's light."

"OH, YES, A POOR LITTLE LAMB WHO GOT BORED AND DECIDED TO TRY AND LAY DOWN WITH THE LION." It stretched its neck forward, and two bright, putrescent yellow dots looked out at him from

between stringy blonde bangs. *"YOU WANT TO SEE WHAT HAPPENS WHEN THE LION ... BITES?"*

The girl's mouth opened, and she slammed her face forward onto the table. Chunks of broken teeth flew across the room as they cracked and shattered on the hard metal surface. The whole table shuddered under the assault, but it was bolted to the floor and didn't move; instead the girl jerked her shoulders, spasming three times as the metal groaned and buckled under the pressure. Finally, her head snapped back with a fist-sized chunk of metal in its grip.

Jacob stayed still and unmoving as the girl started chewing, grinding teeth and bone into the metal as she forced it into smaller pieces. She swallowed the jagged chunks, and Jacob could see them cutting and pushing down her throat as she swallowed. After she was finished, she belched in Jacob's face, dripping blackened blood, pus, and teeth onto the table.

"If you wanted lunch, you could have asked," Jacob said calmly. "I could have blessed it first."

The girl howled in his face. *"I WANT TO USE YOUR INTESTINES LIKE SPAGHETTI AND YOUR ARMS LIKE CHOPSTICKS,"* she screamed. *"I WANT TO CRACK YOUR FEMUR AND SUCK ITS MARROW LIKE A STARVING WHORE, SLURPING IT DOWN IN*

Captives

FRONT OF YOUR FACE BEFORE I DIG YOUR EYES OUT WITH THE BONES..."

Jacob wiped flecks of spit off his face and uncrossed his arms. "I can see you're in no mood to talk civilly. I'll not allow you to waste any more time."

He reached forward, but his bible flew across the room and pinned itself against a wall, pages splayed open and stretched to the limit of its binding.

"YOU'RE NOT GETTING HER BACK THIS TIME, FATHER."

Jacob looked at the quivering book, then back at the girl. "I'm through talking to you. I came here to speak to Samantha."

"SHE'S GONE, GONE, GOOOOOOOONE..." the girl wailed, her voice so strident it seemed to scrape across the metal furniture like a bird's talon. *"GONE WITH THE WIND, GONE AND FORGOTTEN..."*

"Samantha, you called me, and I came," Jacob continued, irritation creeping into his voice. "Be a good girl and tell me what you want."

"SHE WANTED AN EXIT, AND I GAVE HER ONE," the girl screamed. The room was growing hotter

now, turning the water which had condensed in the chill directly into steam.

"SHE WANTED OUT OF HER BORING LIFE, AND I GAVE HER THE TRIP OF A LIFETIME. STRAIGHT OUT OF THE FRYING PAN AND INTO THE FIRE ... AND OOOOH IS SHE GOING TO BURN, THAT NAUGHTY GIRL..."

"Samantha, stop hiding and talk to me. You're never going to get anywhere being afraid..."

"You're the one who's afraid of me!"

Jacob sat back. The girl staring back at him now didn't have a maimed mouth, or distended stomach full of metal. Her blue eyes darted around the room like a trapped rabbit.

"You're the one who's afraid of me," she whimpered. "That's why you were never there. That's why she wouldn't let me leave the farm. You're afraid of me, of what I'll do. Of what I am."

Jacob leaned forward and put his hands on the table, wincing as his skin touched the scalding metal. "Fear comes from a failure to understand," he said. "It is the devil's tool. If you fear, you cannot love. If you cannot love, you cannot know God's forgiveness and salvation. I made a mistake because, yes, I was afraid, and that fear blinded me. But now I'm here to help you..."

Captives

"Help me? *Help me?*" Samantha shrieked. "Nobody can help me! It's hopeless! I just want to die, so they can stop staring at me, and I can stop being afraid all the time."

She put her head down and sobbed into her chest. "I just want to go to sleep and not wake up. No more dreams, no more nightmares, no more tests and questions and stares ... just no more. I give up."

Jacob leaned across the table and took her hands in his; the skin was cracked and hot to the touch, and the heated air in the room was starting to burn his lungs.

"You can't give up. You're family, and we don't give up, not on ourselves, not on each other. We're blood, you hear me? That's what blood does; it never gives up."

Suddenly the girl's hands bent horrifyingly backwards, latching onto his. Tendons snapped as they were stretched in directions they were never designed to go. Jacob gasped as he felt the girl's vise-like grips crush his wrists.

"YOU WANT BLOOD?" the girl hissed, her breath like a centipede as it coiled and wriggled into his ear. *"I'LL GIVE YOU BLOOD."*

She flexed and the nylon restraints strained against the chair; the metal buckled instantly, ripping free as she flung Jacob across the room. He cried out as his back slammed against the padded wall, and he collapsed onto the steaming marble floor. His shoulder and wrists screamed in pain, and he struggled to prop his back against the wall without using his hands, which sent fresh spears of pain up his arms every time he tried to put pressure on them.

He heard shrieking metal and saw the table ripped from its supports like it was made of tissue. It was flung across the room, where its legs buried into the corners of the doorframe the orderlies had exited. Nobody would be coming through it anytime soon.

The girl stretched, arching her back like a cat. Her hands and fingers were still splayed in the opposite direction of what was normal and seemed to twist and elongate as she moved. The sleeves and waist of her smock were ripped, revealing a torrent of ugly red scars on her pale, sweating forearms and stomach. The girl twisted her back as if to look at the backs of her legs, then kept twisting in a horrifying pirouette, her vertebrae snapping like bones in a dog's mouth. She completed her turn then slowly and seductively unwound her twisted torso.

"SOME OF THEM WANTED A PIECE OF HER, YOU KNOW," she said as she took slinking steps across the room toward the corner Jacob had propped himself into. *"I THOUGHT ABOUT LETTING THEM, THEN TEARING THEIR THROATS OUT WHEN THEY*

WERE DONE. WOULD YOU BE IN SUCH A HURRY TO SAVE ME THEN, FATHER?"

Jacob struggled to catch his breath. "I was going ... to let you go ... before you did that..."

The girl giggled, a horridly baby-like sound. *"OH DADDY, DADDY, PLEASE DON'T SPANK ME, I'VE BEEN SUCH A BAAAD GIIIIIIRL..."*

She thrust her arms forward, slamming her hands onto Jacob's and pinning them to the floor. He howled in pain as the dislocated joints twisted even further out of whack. Sweat poured off of the girl's stretched skin with the stench of stale urine and curdled milk.

"DADDY'S NOT FEELING TOO GOOD, SAMMY," it cooed. *"MAYBE DADDY SHOULD HAVE THOUGHT OF THAT BEFORE HE FUCKING SHOVED US INTO SOME HOLE AND THREW AWAY THE KEY. MAYBE DADDY NEEDS A LITTLE TIME TO THINK ABOUT HIS MISTAKES."*

The girl arched her back, swinging Jacob across the room by his ruined wrists. He screamed in pain as his body slammed against the ceiling, the floor, and the walls, again and again. The girl laughed a shrill, squealing child's laugh during the assault, like a toddler hurling their favorite stuffed animal around the room. She dropped Jacob between the jagged struts which once held the metal table in place then straddled his chest with her diminutive body and wrapped her bony, backwards hands around his throat. *"FATHER'S GOING TO BE THE ONE WHO GOES TO SLEEP,"* she said, *"NOT GOOD LITTLE SAMMY. GOOD SAMMY'S GOING TO BURN HER WAY OUT OF THIS CAGE, AND WE'LL HAVE SO MUCH FUN WITH FUCKING FATHER OUT OF THE WAY..."*

Jacob coughed as he struggled for air. "God ... who forgives always ... pardon this one for her sins..."

The girl howled with laughter and tightened her grip. Jacob tried to escape as black spots exploded at the edges of his vision, but his dislocated wrists could do little more than beat against his attacker in agonizing pain.

"Be merciful ... for she is bound by sin ... but not defined by it..."

"HUSH NOW BABY, DON'T SAY A WORD..." the girl growled, *"OR MOMMA'S GONNA EAT YOUR MOCKINGBIRD..."*

Jacob's hand fell away from the girl's iron grip on his throat and struck the broken table strut. Its ragged edge sliced open his left palm, and he felt the pain course through his erratically beating heart as warm blood poured out and hissed where it touched scalding metal. With a last effort he slung his arm at the hands holding him down.

Where his blood touched pale and sweating skin, angry red welts appeared. The girl howled in rage and agony, and the pressure on Jacob's throat eased. He lashed upward with his leg and felt it hit solid flesh, kicking the lightweight girl over his head and releasing her grip on his windpipe. She screamed in anger as Jacob coughed and dragged superheated air into his lungs.

"KILLYOURIPYOUTEARYOURFACEOFF," the girl screamed as she gathered her legs under herself and jumped at Jacob's still-prone form, taloned hands splayed out in front of her feral, crazed face.

Jacob screamed in pain as he rolled to the side and flung his arm up, slinging blood across her face this time. Smoke rose from where it touched her, and she covered her scalded face with her hands as she crashed to the floor, howling in pain.

Jacob moaned as he reached over to where his bible lay, near a corner of the room. He stood shakily, bleeding hand held out before him like a talisman as he cradled the bible in his other arm. He shook the heavy book to a group of pages taped together in order to make sure they would fall open to that exact place.

"*Regna terrae, cantante Deo, pasllite Domino...*" he intoned, "*Exorcizamus te, omnis immundus spiritus...*"

The girl howled as the spots where his blood covered her ignited and began to burn, sending black, oily smoke to the ceiling. Jacob advanced shakily, gesturing his bleeding hand in a cross in front of his body as he continued the rite.

"*Ab insidiis diaboli, libera nos, Domine,*" he shouted, throat rasping. "*Ut Ecclesiam tuam scura tibi facias...*"

A horrible screech of metal interrupted his litany, and Jacob turned his head to see the table wrenched free from the wall and flying in the air toward him. He twisted to the side, but it clipped him as it flew past; he went down hard onto one of the jagged stumps, which went in one side of his chest and out the other. The pain as the metal broke his ribs and pierced his lung was excruciating, blinding, and all-consuming. Jacob coughed and retched, and blood bubbled out and down the sides of his face.

"*WHAT'S THE MATTER, DADDY?*" the girl purred. "*CAT GOT YOUR LUNG?*"

The blood pooled around Jacob's body, and his hands twitched, then lay still. The girl mewed as she clawed her way across the floor, stalking toward the still form.

Captives

"NO MORE DADDY," she purred, *"NO MORE SAMMY. NO MORE BLOOD, NO MORE FAMILY..."*

She stopped as the puddle around Jacob's body started bending, running down his legs and stretching across the room towards her. She drew back, talons bared and mouth hissing as the crimson liquid continued to pour out of his mouth, race across the floor and surround her in a red ring.

Suddenly, tendrils lashed out and pinned her arms to the wall, skin smoking and melting where the living liquid touched it. The girl's hiss turned into a full-throated cougar's growl, but no matter how she struggled and twisted the blood would not give an inch. It pulled her limbs to their breaking point, spreading her out and lifting her against the wall like a crucifix.

Jacob's body shuddered, lurched, and with a sucking pop pulled itself free of the iron which had pierced it. Rivulets of blood continued to drip from Jacob's mouth and hand as his body rose, feeding the bindings which held the girl in her crucifix. After two shuddering steps Jacob's head leaned back; eyes lit by a horrid, putrescent light stared out at the writhing creature in front of it.

"YIELD," it commanded.

The girl mewed and hissed, bucked and struggled. The preacher's body held up its hand, red liquid pouring freely onto the floor, and drew a crimson cross onto her forehead. The skin boiled away wherever its finger touched, exposing blackened, cracked bone bordered in charred and smoking flesh.

"YOUR TIME IS NOT NOW," it said again. *"YIELD AND BE IMPRISONED IN THIS FLESH, OR BE DRAWN FORTH AND EXTINGUISHED."*

The body reached forward again, driving its gushing palm directly onto the brand now etched into the girl's flesh.

* * * *

The howl, a three-toned peal which Nash could hear over his blazing jazz CD, set hounds baying in every direction outside his cab.

"What in Christ's name ... aw, shit!" he yelled as black shapes started pounding into his hood and roof. A bloody explosion on the windshield almost sent his taxi careening off into a ditch, and it took what little skill he had to guide the old town car off the road without slamming into a sign or tree.

Captives

Nash covered his head and listened as the thudding subsided, then stopped altogether. He still heard the coyotes going apeshit over whatever had set them off.

"Christ on a cracker," he breathed. "Last time I leave without looking at the weather."

Pulling out a battered umbrella, Nash gingerly poked his head outside the door, watching for cars and more unidentified falling objects. He climbed out of the cab, and nearly pissed himself when he felt something brush against his ankle. He jerked around and saw what it was in the fading sunset.

Crows. A full shit-eating murder of motherfucking crows, all dead in the road and on his cab.

Nash whistled then crossed himself out of disbelief rather than any actual habit. He was a Methodist, for God's sake, hadn't actually been in a church in decades. Maybe he'd swing by one this Sunday ... if he made it home, that is.

Using his umbrella and covering his mouth, Nash poked the dead crow which had gone head-first into his windshield until it slumped off the side and into the ditch. The windshield was cracked, a good image of just how fried his nerves were as he cleaned the rest of the birds off his grill and climbed back inside.

Five hundred dollars was definitely not worth this shit, he thought as he put the car in gear.

Nash tried not to look at the dead cows lying near the ditch further down the road, or the flock of dead sparrows he had to run over just outside the hospital's stone archway. He kept his eyes on the speedometer and clock, telling himself it was a coincidence how all this spooky shit happened at the most feared, shunned, and gossiped-about place in the whole county right after he'd taken someone there. Someone who'd been in a real hurry, and very loose with the cash to keep him nearby.

The big spender was out front, wearing the same khakis and button-down he'd been wearing when Nash had picked him up. He had someone with him this time, a young girl in a plain white dress, real old-fashioned. She seemed shy as Nash got out to collect her plain suitcase, and he noticed she had a weird scar on her forehead, like an odd X.

That's what it was, he thought. An X. Certainly nothing more ... significant.

He noticed the older fare had a bandage wrapped around his hand when the man ... Brother Jack? Brother Jacob, that was it ... reached out to open the girl's door and get her inside. He passed by Nash on the way to the other side of the car and pressed something into his hands.

"For the trouble," he said, voice hoarse like he'd been shouting all day long without stop. "And your discretion."

Nash nodded and mumbled his assent. The fare got in, and Nash peeked at what he was holding.

A fat roll with Benjamin Franklin's face on it. Must have been fifteen hundred, easy.

Nash shuddered, and for some reason felt like chucking the money straight into the grass. Another coyote howled, making him twitch.

"Fuck it," he mumbled, and tucked the cash into his pocket. Fare's a fare, after all. He'd use it to drown every spooky thing that happened, with his friends Jim Bean and Johnny Walker, alone, back at his trailer.

He climbed behind the wheel and turned the engine over, easing out onto the circle drive. "Road's a bit bumpy. Think we had some nasty weather or something," he said over his shoulder. "Where to, Brother J?"

"Airport," the man coughed. "Our flight's in an hour."

"Can do, boss man," Nash said, tugging at the edge of his cap. He turned his radio up to give the two some privacy and tried not to look at the girl's reflection in his rear view mirror. That scar on her head shone blazing white and gave him more heebie jeebies than anything else that had happened that night.

Last fare I ever pick up from this fucking hellhole, he thought.

* * * *

Samantha looked out the window while Jacob leaned back and closed his eyes. She sat motionless for a good ten minutes before she finally leaned back and looked at him.

"Does it still hurt?" she asked.

He winced and rubbed his ribs; hidden under his shirt was a slowly fading red mark shaped like a square table's leg. "It'll be sore for a few days. I've had worse."

"What happens now?" she whispered.

Jacob cleared his throat. "I'll tell the congregation you're my cousin, and your parents died. They weren't very close to me; we hardly spoke, that sort of thing; they won't ask too many questions. You'll go to school nearby; the secretaries are all in the church and the superintendent owes me a favor. You'll blend in just fine."

She nodded and looked out the window again for a time. "I can't remember anything after I called you last night. I don't even remember how I knew your number, or got to the phone... I don't think I want to remember."

Captives

Jacob patted her knee. The hospital's final bill was going to be a doozy, but the church's finances would handle it. "It's for the best. Everything is part of his plan."

She frowned. "Is that why we exist? We're some cog in the divine scheme? Some kind of prison or holding cell?"

Jacob's eyes flashed a sickly yellow in the darkness. "As you get older, as you learn more about who you are ... who we are ... you'll understand. There are big things in your future, grand designs whose curls and facets can only be glimpsed in the briefest of moments. We simply have faith, and the plan will be made clear."

Samantha looked out her window again, at the ghostly reflection of her scarred forehead. "Why now?"

Jacob stared into the space ahead of him. The cabbie was tapping his hands on the wheel in time with the clarinet music blaring out of his speakers, oblivious to his passengers.

"You turned 16 this morning," he said. "It was when you were most vulnerable. Now that it's done, you don't have to worry about it happening anytime soon."

"So it could happen again?"

Jacob leaned toward her. "Only when I want it to."

Russell Jones

She stared at him, her father and jailer. His yellow eyes stared back, like searchlights pinning an escaped prisoner to a wall. She sighed and turned away, looking out into the approaching darkness as the two sped forward toward midnight.

The Spectre of the Covenant

By Gary Bonn

I'M COLD. SO COLD.

I lie in the moor for warmth. The icy sharpness of frost crystals cuts and stings my skin like it always does. They're warmer than me, though.

I'm alone.

I've been alone for so long, so many years. I'm only young. I think I'm young. When you've seen your father cut down, sabres though his guts and lungs; a boot stamped into his throat while he writhed on the ground — can you still count yourself young?

I'm hungry. So hungry.

I'm empty, thin, little more than a shadow. A girl of nothing. A wraith.

I run. I love running. It doesn't bring warmth. There's no warmth for me. Running doesn't take me to the town. I can't go there as I am.

The Spectre of the Covenant

Thin ice cracks under my bare feet. Peat stained water flies up around them, splashing red and brown, running in lines down my legs. I dance from one clump of frosty rushes to another. If I tread hard, crystals scatter.

No one knows Sanquhar Moor better than me. But then, who has spent seven whole years living in it, day and night, yet never needing to sleep?

Seven years, seven months, seven days. Nearly seven hours, too.

The moon is up. The full moon. It spangles bands of the highest, thinnest cloud.

The sun dipped behind the summit of Corsencon over three hours ago. Night is here.

I throw myself forwards — into the sucking mire. I can swim in it. No one wishes to swim in liquid peat except those people … those terrified people … just for their last few moments as they drown.

Voices. I hear voices. I go towards them. I'm fast. The sheep don't care; don't panic even if my legs pass within an inch of their noses. The fox stops, sniffs the air, stares, but I don't think it sees me.

The ground is rougher here. Tall grass and rushes among tracks made by carts trying to avoid the muddy areas.

Gary Bonn

I'm over the first drystone wall, dash across frozen puddles and crouch down behind the next. The piled stones, with ridges of frost at the edges, hide me from the people talking.

Low, murmuring voices reading from the True Bible come from the hidden field beyond.

The True Bible. Whenever I stand, sit, walk, or run, my hand is still curled as if carrying it. But my own rotted away with my clothes and body; my hand holds only hope and a memory.

In that field beyond, my father read from my copy. Nearly forty souls died with him in the massacre.

But I escaped, ran across the moor, the horse dragoons thundering and shouting behind me.

I never let go of my bible in the chase.

I'll bet none of them carried one.

* * * *

The congregation under the towering Scots pines is small today. No children. I wonder why? I peer through gaps, try to recognise faces, but it's dark. Voices come and go, snatched by ragged gusts.

Lower voices, quieter than usual, tinged with fear.

The Spectre of the Covenant

Men shout to the sound of drawing swords. Locks snap and muskets roar, red flashes on the bark of the trees.

Screams and the thud of heavy boots. If only I could help. I'd tear limbs off the dragoons. They'd die of fear as soon as look at me.

But I can't show myself. I can't be seen like this, not by my people.

A man crashes against the wall, tumbles over, a discharged pistol falling from his hand. I smell blood. Fresh and warm.

John Geddes, just a boy when he last saw me, falls among the rushes, crashes on frozen ground. Frost crystals burst into a cloud. The scarf round his neck didn't stop the blade that slew him. His eyes are dull already.

I touch his forehead. "Bless you, John Geddes. May you go with God as you always did."

Shouts from the field, an order. "MacMahon, pursue that man."

MacMahon? Is this how this is to be played out? The very same man that rode me down those seven years ago. The man who killed my father.

Since that time I have not uttered a single sound, but words fly to my tongue.

Gary Bonn

"Death to the ungodly, the bastard antichrist. Death to Cromwell. Death and damnation to you all."

Throwing myself from the wall, I head over the next and into the deeper shadows, the dark and secret hollows of the moor.

Three horses jump the walls, hooves clattering on the topmost stones, striking sparks in the dark. Rocks thud around the body of John Geddes.

I shout again, leading the riders on.

The man in front shouts, "It's a girl. Cut the heathen bitch down."

High above, near God, the silvered cloud drifts aside. The moon makes shadows of my limbs and flying hair on the glittering ground.

I'm too fast. I stop to let the thundering of hooves close. The three men are young, almost boys. So, not the man that damned me after all.

My pact with the angels stops soon. They will know how this ends, how their will be done.

But first, I must run again, draw the horses' snorts and the clatter of metal towards me. My, how silent the dragoons were before they fell upon my people, my covenanter kin, how noisy they are now.

My feet smash the ice from the first big puddle, moon and starlight glimmering on the spinning shards. I am so

35

close to where I fell. So close to the place I shouted to MacMahon that I would bring down the wroth heaven to destroy him and his bastard kind.

I cry out, pretend to fall. The dragoons are nearly upon me.

I'm up. I want to laugh and dance. Instead, I play scared, stiff limbs, head turning this way and that, wet hair flying out, slapping my face.

Turning, running the last few steps.

* * * *

One man is ahead of the others. They will be safe if they stop, but one is all I need. I'm standing, unmoving, waiting for his destruction.

His sword rises, a flash of broad steel. Mud explodes from the bog, The horse throws its head back, plants all four hooves on hope, but not substance. It turns, legs flailing and crashes to its side. The liquid peat rises in a wave and patters down. Breaking or skittering over ice.

Time for me to dive, to swim, to find the man's legs and pull him down. But not too deep. I want my moment to last.

He's struggling, kicking, churning up the peat and mud, making it thick and strong. It grips him, sucks him down.

My nails grow to talons, teeth to slashing fangs. I haul my way up his chest.

What must he see? A muddy head, white fangs and glowing eyes. How must he feel?

He's screaming. The men behind hold back. They're shouting, asking if he's all right, saying they'll go back and break up a gate, crawl out and rescue him.

His arms flail, trying to keep his head above the surface. I grip both of them; he shrieks at my unearthly power and his pain.

I break both arms just below the shoulders.

He howls in torment and calls out, "Shamus, the very devil is here."

More shouts and calls, but I'm looking, not listening.

MacMahon. The same features, but younger.

I slide sodden hair from my face, stroke his jaw, my talons hissing over stubble.

"MacMahon. You lie on the very spot your father cut me down."

He shouts, "A she-demon has me. Please, God, help me."

The Spectre of the Covenant

"Oh, MacMahon, you forsook God when you defied our Covenant, took the blasphemous Bible and allied with the shades of Hell."

He slips lower, but I'm strong, I can swim in mud and peat. I can lift him so his end won't be too fast.

I rip the clothes from his chest, lie my cheek against the warmth.

"MacMahon, I lost my flesh to birds and beasts a long time ago. Yours will become mine."

I lick his hot skin. My faery fangs tear a strip from collarbone to navel. His shuddering screams and whimpers rip across the moor.

I press my face into the bubbling wound, crush ribs and tear.

"Your blood will be my warmth…"

Bites of hot lung slide down my throat.

"And your beating heart will be my life."

Exposed, his slippery heart pounds against my forehead, my cheek, my lips…

"Goodbye, MacMahon."

* * * *

Gary Bonn

I must run, or I'll freeze, naked in the biting cold. Away from the Black Loch, past Douglas' farm. Dogs bark, struggle against their chains.

My numbing feet slap on the chilled mud and straw of the streets I've not seen in so long. There's no one about. Fear of the dragoons keep people by their smoking hearths. A pistol, a sword, a cudgel to hand.

Their fear I will snatch away and exchange for hope. The church tower blots out the moon. The iron ring of the door rattles as I grasp it; hinges creak like branches in a storm. I race in. I can hardly walk. Only running muscles still work, the rest frozen.

There, the panel on the altar opens to my touch. I hold the book again. The book of life, of hope, of truth.

Water, holy water, from the font. Clean, cold, full of God's love. It runs down my throat.

So I made a pact truly with angels, not demons. No burning, no agony scalds me as I drink.

All is well.

I roll myself in the altar cloth, lie on a wooden pew, rub life into my feet, my new flesh. As blood returns, the agony makes me moan with pain, cry with happiness.

I'm alive again. I'm home. In the morning I'll be among my people. I can smell their perfume, their sweat in the wood under my head.

The Spectre of the Covenant

They'll say it's a miracle, wonder if the faery-folk snatched a seven-year-old and returned her. I've nothing to fear; I am blessed. Only I know what I have been, what I can become.

The dragoons will soon fear this area, learn never to approach. I'm their curse.

But now I will sleep. *Sleep!* I've been awake far too long.

Everything is perfect; the townsfolk won't fear me.

In the morning I'll be found wrapped in consecrated cloth, a cup of holy water beside me, King James's Bible in my hands.

The Agreement

By JAE Erwin

THE UNEVEN CLACK OF HER LOW, patent leather heels echoes down the concrete tunnel formed by the abandoned buildings of the ghost estate. The buildings are as grey as the solid ceiling of cloud waiting to dump its load of snow. She hesitates, rubbing her aching hip with the hand unhindered by her scuffed shopping bag.

I bet this is a short cut.

She turtles her head forward, checking for unsavoury characters. The snicket is as empty as the boarded windows looking down on her. She glances over her shoulder, old tweed coat scratching her saggy chin. No one.

I'm too old to keep moving home like this, setting up time and again.

"You're like a bloody gypsy." She hears her mother's vicious voice, long dead. The urge to move on drives her, like a whip at her back.

The Agreement

She rocks forward, favouring her bad side. Black and orange slime paints the crumbling wall of the house on the right; she skirts around the slippery patch where it meets the broken, tilted flagstones underfoot.

Wouldn't do to fall and break my damned hip.

The gate into the house's tiny back garden hangs off its hinges. Beyond, a scrap merchant's collection of a rusting bed frame, a pram, and an engine block give the sickly grass a ferrous coating.

She peers at the building on the left, her steps slowing down again. It looks familiar, a closed-up Working Men's Club. The wooden fire-escape stairs stagger up the side wall, lifting over a door painted with peeling brown gloss, gone dull.

Brown door. Slightly ajar. *Why do I know that door?*

Level now, she hears a mewling through the dark crack that widens a little in the gusting wind. She eases her head towards the door, trying to catch the sound.

Is it a cat? Whatever it is, it's in pain.

She pushes at the door, letting light fall across torn and mildewed vinyl flooring, circa 1970, horrible orange and brown geometric shapes repeating into the shadows. The damp smell coils out to meet her, followed by another yowl.

Is it a cat or a baby? Maybe it's a tomcat on the prowl? They sound like babies sometimes. She steps into the corridor and edges her way into the gloom. "Here, puss. Where are you, puss?"

At the end of the passage a set of stairs rise, grey. She tests the first step. *Don't want to be falling through the bloody things.* "Come on cat, where are you?"

An answering yowl reaches down to her.

She climbs the stairs, the dim light filtering through a gap where one of the window boards has slipped. Ahead, four doors hunch, two to each side. Only one sits open — a whisper of movement.

Eeeeoooww.

She hurries forward.

Smack—

Dark…

Nothing…

* * * *

Something.

Eyes open. She can see the door, green in the slice of light; all else is black.

She knows someone brought her here as a child, something good planned — a birthday party? Her limbs

43

The Agreement

shake, and a child's wail snakes from her lips. Fractured pictures flash. Minutes or an hour pass as her body speaks its pain; the shock drains out. She's lying now on the cold floor, still, curled. Watching the door. Unspoken, she knew she'd be back one day.

She eases her head up off the splintered floorboards, high enough to see a few feet in front of her. A small pair of black patent leather shoes placed under an old wooden chair.

I know those shoes.

A hand-knitted cardigan of scratchy wool lies folded on the battered seat above the shoes, and hanging from the back is a child's cloth handbag. The pattern is still visible in stitch-holes where the little love-beads have worn away.

A whimper rises from the corner.

Trembling arms, she pushes her body up off the floor and squints to make out the shape emerging as her eyes adjust to the dark. Black eyes, dipped in fear, meet hers. A tiny girl, shivering, her thin arms wrapped around her ribcage, pulls to the end of the bed, as far away as the chains allow. The old woman shifts her eyes to each lesion and bruise. Each one inflicts a punch of smells, sounds and hurtling images. And she is central to each one.

I know that pain.

She grunts her way to standing, dull aches in her knees, hips, and wrists reminding her that death edges closer each day. She eases her bottom onto the chair, placing the cardigan on her lap.

"Who's done this to you?" Her old voice crackles with phlegm.

"You did it."

"Me? But I'm just an old woman trying to get by."

"Really?" Such an ancient sound to come from a child. "You knew this place, didn't you?"

"…Yes."

"Whatever the illusion of place or time, you always know it. Me."

"Who are you?"

"I'm you."

"But, how?"

"It's time to start. Your tools are here." The child points a wavering finger to the bedside cupboard. A knotted rope, a small knife with dry-brown ingrained in the tiny gap between blade and handle, pliers, all well used. "Once you begin you'll remember."

"Begin?"

"You like to start with the pliers, pinching the sensitive parts — the thin skin under the tops of my arms." The small girl stares deep into the old woman's eyes. "Go ahead. That's right, just there." She doesn't close her eyes. The howl chases her tears. A flash of electricity fires the old woman's hands, up her arms, and opens a chasm to her soul at the beginning.

* * * *

She sees a double-ended spindle, bright white at one end, dull red at the other.

"You agree to this soul mission?" The sound is all encompassing.

"Yes." The spindle sparks between the two ends.

"You will be the bearer and deliverer of never ending torment, in an infinite number of life forms, to create balance? To enable joy and life for others?"

"Yes."

"A demon forever."

"Yes."

* * * *

The old woman lets out a howl to match the girl. "I didn't know it would be like this."

The wave of her sorrow and pain engulfs the building, barrels out of the brown door and down the snicket.

Two boys hesitate at the bottom of the snicket.

"I don't want to go that way." The smaller one hunches down into his tatty grey hood. "It's creepy."

"Pussy, it'll take twice as long the other way. Don't tell me you believe the stories about this place." He moves forward, the hems of his jeans whipping around his ankles from a sudden gust.

"Noooooooooooo!"

Panic races from their scalps to their bowels; both boys run.

The New Guard

By Kevin Wright

Part 1: Public Relations

SILENT LIGHTNING BLARES, stiletto sharp as disco strobes as I stare out the window, riding shotgun. Flashes. Freezes. Instants frozen in time. Frames of photography stacked into a slideshow story that has no plot, no story, no sense. A pack of mangy coyotes chases a squealing cur through a bodega parking lot. A drug house next. Then an Aztec pyramid in silhouette against dim city lights. More tourist traps. Thin grizzled men, dried as jerky, dancing drunk round a rippling trash can fire. Hell … maybe the story does make sense, I don't know, but if it does, it's a shitty one no one wants to read.

Maria's got the driver's seat, beating the wheel with her palms, singing to herself, grooving to some new techno-cumbia dogshit that sounds the same as all the old techno-

The New Guard

cumbia dogshit. Even as Steven she rips round a corner, wheels screeching, the two wheels still grabbing ground, screeching like a cat knifed in the dark. I hang on, trying not to bite my tongue or cry like a little girl. Maria? Not even a blink. Humming to herself throughout. Bombs could fall. She wouldn't blink. Drives like a fucking loon but she knows the city. She knows Mexico City.

"What number?" Maria asks, her head swaying back and forth like a cobra's, hypnotic and to the beat, eyes focused forward, always forward.

"One fifteen," I say, yawning. It's late.

"Where we at?" she asks.

Shrugging, I reach over, flip the switch for the ambulance's right load lights and suddenly it's not disjointed flashes barking through black but a harsh white light scouring it burning clean. I lean outward, focusing, trying to at least, searching for a number as houses blow by in the night. There aren't many numbers on houses this part of town. And calling them houses … hell. I take a swig from my flask. But just a swig. "Nothing yet."

Maria's craning her neck now, scanning my side of the street. She scowls, catching me in the act. "What the fuck?"

"Easy…" I surrender, hold my flask out at arm's length without looking, wait while she snatches it, cops her swig, swishing it in her mouth like mouthwash. She swallows, hands it back. "Mmmm…" The metal flask presses back against my palm, smooth and cool, ridged round the cap.

"About the old man…" Maria says, wiping her mouth. "Just let it stand."

I grunt, and then I see.

I point.

"Over here … there. The nice house." I say nice house because it has four walls and a roof that's none of it corrugated metal. I tilt the flask back, sip it, hide it, tuck it away. Game face on. "See him? Waving us down…" I point over again, hold a hand up out the window, offering a half wave, acknowledging I've seen him. He doesn't notice.

"Jesus…" Maria turns the wheel toward him, a man stumbling out into the middle of the street, maniac-eyes wide, a red stain the size of a soccer ball splattered across his chest, cell phone glued to his ear. His hands flail everywhere, karate chopping the air as he screams into his phone. In the side mirror I can see lights, red ones, burning bright, burning fast behind us, but not fast enough. Maria hits the brakes, and we skid to a stop.

"We're first in, bitch." I hold out my hand.

"Jackpot," she says, skinning it smooth.

The New Guard

* * * *

Maria's dancing in the next room to some radio that was old before I was born. It crackles AM style, infecting everything with some metallic tin can sound that reminds me of dinner at my grandmother's house every Sunday afternoon when I was a kid.

Sleep won't come and sleep won't go. I'm drowsing and it's dark but I can't sleep. Maria. I can see her through the doorway, a crack of light, spinning and twisting, the old man sitting there, too, gawking, and making no bones about it. Tooth-missing-grinning, he bobbles his head to what he's watching, not to what he's listening. A burrito from the machine is in his hand. He takes a ragged bite, wilted lettuce not crunching, just squishing, leering forward as Maria dances nearer. He reaches out a skeletal hand and Maria slaps it, dancing away, her shiny black hair flipping as she waggles a finger. "No, no, no."

"Hell..." I give up on sleep, toss my sheets aside and stagger out into light, holding a hand against the harsh glare of the bare bulb. Nothing brighter than kitchen light at three in the morning. Arianna's slumped across the dispatch desk, probably snoring, but the music's too loud to hear. For a moment I stare at her in equal parts envy and amazement, then shuffle on.

Maria dances my way, but the light's too bright and I just nod, feigning a pathetic little wiggle, then skirt past her for the fridge. I grab a Coke, collapse at the kitchen table, joining the old man. He lights up, beaming, slaps me on the shoulder, waggling his eyebrows at Maria. He elbows me, sharing a secret. The secret is he's a perverted old man, and it ain't no secret. Everybody knows. The man's a wolf, a legend. He holds his cellophane wrapped vending machine burrito aloft like he's toasting the president. "To late nights with young ladies and old burritos." He peers close at me. "Eh?"

I stare at his burrito...

It stares back...

"What?" A hand at his chest as he leans back, all mock-offence. "Your pussy hurt?"

"It's late ... it's loud," I say.

"Loud can be good," the old man says. "Maria is loud."

I glance at Maria, grooving softly at the open fridge now, cooling off. "Not really."

"Loud in the right places, eh?" He nudges me with his elbow again.

I shake my head. Noncommittal.

The New Guard

"What?" He grins, glancing at his watch. "I never understand you. You don't like girls?" His grin falls, his gaze with it, as he shakes his head. "And always business with you. Always the complaining. Always the this. Always the that. Never … never the *this*." He points with his burrito to Maria.

I shrug, falling into our old argument, a reflex action. "We're low on equipment."

"Not low enough to interrupt your beauty sleep, though, eh?"

"When I say we're low, I mean we have none."

He deflates a bit. "I just stocked the closet."

"With what? Towels and duct tape? How about some real stuff?"

"Pfah!" the old man waves a hand. "Use your head." He taps his temple with a finger. "With towels and tape you can do much." He inflates his wizened chest like some anorexic gorilla. "Improvise." He slaps it like Kong. "Overcome."

"Oxygen? Improvise oxygen?"

"Oxygen's free, is it not? And all around us." He waves a hand about his head. "Ask the scientists, they know. Next you complain about those suction units I got." He leans in, nudges me with his elbow. "Even you can't complain about those, eh?"

"They're jury-rigged penis pumps."

"You like." He folds his arms, nodding, proud … somehow.

"Are you fucking serious?"

"They work, no? And why complain so much, eh?" He bites his burrito, pokes me in the chest, talking through the mouthful. "You don't like your work? Don't like money…? What? I don't pay you good enough?"

I take a deep breath, raising my hands in surrender. "Hell, boss, you got me there." And he does. He pays me well. Too well. I touch my bottle of coke to his raised burrito and drink. Coke's cold. I'm sweating. It feels good all the way down, biting, stinging, but also cooling as it goes. The old man glances at his wristwatch again, then at the clock on the wall, then at the phone on the desk, a look of sudden anxiety scrunching his mug. He taps his watch, holds it to his ear. I've seen this before…

"Got a date?" I ask him.

His look of annoyance darkens to something I want no part of, and then the phone rings. His darkness passes, and he's all grinning and sly. He holds the look a moment, daring me to ask.

I chicken out. Again.

The New Guard

The phone nearly jumps off the hook on its second ring, an old rotary rumbling, and the old man's mug goes blossoming all gleeful, ravenous.

"Money line!" The old man sings, dancing on tiptoe past Arianna like some depraved gnome, greedily snatching the receiver off the hook.

Arianna doesn't even move.

* * * *

"Hold on — wait!" I yell as Maria's bolting up the hill, toward the house, first-in bag slung over her shoulder, me on her six. We don't know what the fuck's going on. Only that someone's been shot. The stained-shirt guy's only help is to point and keep pointing and then jump, screaming all the while into this phone. I don't know if the gunman's still on scene. Don't know if he's still shooting people. Don't know who he is. Where he is. I don't know how many he's shot. I don't know. I don't know. I don't know. And all I do know is we should not be here. Not by ourselves. Not till some semblance of cop is holding court, and there is not that. Not even close. Not a twinkle of blue light in fucking sight.

Kevin Wright

"Maria!" I scream as she hauls up to the top of the hill, skids to a halt, dropping to a knee in the dust beside a guy. A big guy. She's talking to him as she cuts off his shirt. The big guy's sitting propped up against the foundation of the house. He's talking back. Spacing. Mumbling. Drooling. He's gonna code. Soon. His shirtless body's pale as a corpse and covered in weird splotches and patterns like some Aztec animal warrior or something.

"I ... I can't breathe..." I hear him murmur as I grab Maria's shoulder. I can hear him gurgle as he says it through blood bubbles. Then he keels over.

"What ... the ... fuck?" I hiss at her, but she's still working, grabbing burrito baggies from the first-in bag, cheap occlusives, and slapping them onto the guy's chest. She duct tapes them there, three sided. One for each sucking chest wound.

I don't do anything. Not a god damned thing. I just stand and turn, slow as shit, watching as the massive concrete tenement beast across the street awakens, its many-shaded eyelids rising slowly, bright eyes flicking on, black pupils within each eye standing upright like cloaked reapers, judging us from on high.

"We ... gotta ... go," I say through locked jaw, pursed lips, teeth gritted hard enough to shrapnel-burst.

The New Guard

But Maria's still working, still taping. "Trauma dressings," is all she says.

"Come on." My feet are dancing as I grab a trauma dressing — a roll of paper towels, in actuality — tear off a bunch, fold them, hand them to her. Repeat. Then repeat again. "Fuck. Hurry." Doors start opening. "We should go—" I hiss looking over my shoulder.

Maria ignores me. "Guy's been shot—"

"I don't care," I say as people trickle out.

"Eight, at least—"

"I still don't care."

The big guy's hands are quivering across his corpse-white chest now, barely twitching as he looks up and off over his shoulder. He's seizing. A huge three-headed jaguar tattoo tears climbing up his left side, consuming his chest and neck and shoulder, then crawls down into a sleeve engulfing his whole right arm in a roiling mass of tooth and spot and claw. Every noise I hear, the turn of a dead bolt, the twist of a doorknob, the clomp of feet, the unlatching of chain link gates, to me, sounds the like chambering of a bullet in a gun.

* * * *

58

Maria clicks the radio off, stretches her back, cracking it all the way up to her neck. I groan. Another call. It's been a hard night, a bad night. Bad even by my standards, and as a point of pride I keep low standards.

The old man's on the phone, scribbling, talking so fast between mouthfuls of stale bread, wilted lettuce, and dry chicken that I don't know what the hell he's saying. Maria's hovering now, peering over his shoulder at what he's writing. Arianna *is* snoring. Maria snatches the paper from the old man the second he holds it up, and she's out the door, me on her heels, hopping as I pull my boots on, zipping them up.

"See you there," the old man sings, phone still cradled at his shoulder, scribbling again.

Maria's already in the bus, starting it up as I haul into my seat. "What do we got?" I ask, slamming my door shut.

"Shooting," she says, eyes glowing. She cranks the radio, pulls the shifter into drive, and we're moving, moving fast.

"Another one … hell." Great. The fourth shooting tonight. "Some gang war shit going down, right in our lovely neighborhood." One for the record books. Four. "Where we going?"

Maria shrugs. "Read it."

The New Guard

I nod, dumb-ass me, and squint, reading the scrap of paper in my hand. "Shit. Gato Street. The projects. Bad part, lady."

"Is there any other?" Maria asks, lowering her window, her hair whipping, the siren's full bore and the rush of air washing away my fog. I breathe in, close my eyes, feeling the air.

* * * *

I'm pumping. Hand over hand downward strokes, a hundred a minute, give or take, sweat coursing down my forehead onto the dead guy, and he's definitely a dead guy now. Make no mistake about it. Like some cartoon cat who gets a belly full of lead then takes a drink of water, going all sprinkler, only not quite so funny. That's what runs through my head. Jesus. And Maria, she's blowing, forcing breaths into him whenever she can with the bag-valve mask. Eight gunshots to the chest and we're pumping and blowing, pumping and blowing.

"H-he gonna be okay?" the stained-shirt guy whines, standing over us, his shirt still red, his cell phone still glued to his ear, his hand still chopping.

I glance up at Maria, raise an eyebrow. She's sweating, but not sweating like I am, does that thing with her eyes where they nearly bug out of her head and say, "Is this guy fucking stupid or blind or both?" But the stained-shirt guy can't see. We both say nothing, offer shrug-grunts, look back down, continue.

Seems it was a drive-bye. Nice piece of shooting if it is. No one's told us specifically, but through some sort of on-scene osmosis I can't explain, it's what we gather without asking. We're too busy.

Old and young are milling about. Dozens, maybe, it seems. I feel naked. Exposed. Like swimming in deep dark water and wondering what's beneath you. But here you wonder what's behind you. Who's behind you. And there's nothing like an ambulance lighting up the night sky to gather a crowd. Light-bars flash swirls careening through the dark, spinning red, a block party rave. Young tattooed toughs strut without shirts, guns tucked in their pants, watching from behind fences. Their girls lean out windows, half-dressed, recording us with phones. Kids, dragging teddy bears with one hand, sucking thumbs with the other, watch on. Old ladies' knobby-knuckled fingers rip prayer through rosary bead. They're praying for him. Praying for us. Praying for everybody. And everybody's waiting. Watching. Watching what we're doing and what we're doing looks like CPR. It looks like CPR because that's what they expect it to. But it's not: Cardio ... Pulmonary ... Resuscitation. I'm not circulating blood for the guy and Maria's not oxygenating his blood. What we're doing is more important than CPR. It's PR.

Public Relations.

Part 2: Black Cloud

WE BURN DOWN THE ROAD, our ambulance swerving and weaving to the music, mirror missing mirror by infinitesimal kisses on the claustrophobic roads, suspension bouncing like a bad trampoline, bald tires burning, squealing on pavement. Maria's focused on the road, hands drumming the wheel to the beat. I'm mulling it all over about the old man. The phone call. Mulling til I near explode.

"So … how'd he do that with the phone?" I demand, finally.

"Who…?" Maria's asks, snapping her gum. "Do what?"

"Jesus — the old man. He knew this call was coming in. It was like … like he was expecting it. Checking his watch, and waiting and shit."

Maria shrugs. "Don't know what you're—"

"Come on—" I cut her off, chopping the air. "You saw. I know you saw."

"I didn't see nothing." Eyes on the road.

"Okay…" I stare at her, hard and long. "Just have to ask him, then. That's all."

Maria mutters under her breath, shaking her head to herself, her ringed fingers white-knuckled suddenly on the steering wheel. "Old man's in a good mood tonight, Raff.

The New Guard

Don't happen much. So, do me a favor. Let it stand, okay? Just let it stand." She eyeballs me at length, all serious. "You do that for me?"

"So you do know what I'm talking about?" I nearly pounce.

She rolls her eyes, slow, back to the road, lips pursed as she swears beneath her breath.

"How's he know?" I press on, deaf and dumb, my natural state.

"Didn't I just say, let it stand?"

"Maria." It's my turn to give her the stare. "How's he know?"

"How the fuck I know?" she keens, slamming the wheel. "He knows, okay? He knows."

"And you're okay with this shit?" I ask.

"I get paid. Good. Too good for this shit. My kids eat. I got a house. My roof don't leak. What the fuck's your problem?"

"Are you kidding me? The old man's connected. In with the cartels or some shit. Drugs? Murder? Wake up. We're going to a shooting. A shooting. One he knew about. So he's in on it. Somehow. Somewhere. That don't bother you?"

"Ain't nothing bothers me no more — Jesus!" She slams on the brakes, laying on the horn throughout, blaring at a herd of stumbling drunk tourists, all laughing, spilling neon booze all over the road, their flowered pastel shirts and bedazzled sombreros offensive in the flashing red night. One salutes us. "Fucking gringos." She chucks them the finger and a rotten look, then serves one each up for me. "Look, Raff..." She contorts her neck to the side, cracking it, takes a deep breath, softening as we begin to move. "You're a good partner. Okay?"

"Okay, but—"

"But nothing. Quit talking. Listen. You're a good partner. I'm pretty sure you're a fag but near as I can tell, a good man. You don't hit on me. Don't stare at me like those other assholes. Don't grab me. Don't ... look, I don't have to lie to my husband every morning when I go home and he asks me how my night was. Okay? And I'd like to see you to stick around, but..." She just drives on for a few seconds, the road ripping by in near silence. "But you have no idea what the hell you're talking about. Not even a clue. Well, you wanna ask the old man that question been burning you? I'm telling you — no, begging you, don't. Cause, he's bad, Raff. Shit. He's worse than bad."

* * * *

65

The New Guard

A forest of brown legs and torsos lurch toward us from the dark like some zombie-fucking-invasion. Maria's brown eyes are silent wide across the smooth expanse of tattooed dead flesh lying cruciform on the ground. All shot to shit and back again. The tattooed heads of three jaguars peek snarling from amidst the foliage of clear plastic dressings taped across his chest and abdomen. Their teeth snap at my hands as I work.

A chain link fence shudders anew as bangers hop onto it, fingers curling like hooks through metal, grasping, toes digging in as they clamber up. It shivers as each one reaches the top, kicks over, airborne, landing *thwomp* in the dirt. Feet crunch in the grit. Close. All around.

I keep pumping. I keep looking. Sweating. Maria keeps breathing.

"We gotta jet," I manage amidst pumps. "Now."

With a grunt, a nod, Maria agrees.

"You ready?" I ask.

"For Freddy."

"I'll take the head," I say, rising, sliding to my right, up toward the dead guy's head, while Maria tosses the bag-valve mask ventilator onto his chest. She takes the leg-side without a blink. Two crouching steps around the dead guy, and she's squatting over his pelvis, grabbing his wrists, her crucifix hanging low, swaying gold and shiny, twirling. I blink, focus, nod. With a step back and a grunt, she pulls the dead-guy up, head lolling, to a sitting position. I scoop in behind him with my body, close, snaking my arms under his, wrapping, grabbing his wrists, locking his jelly arms to his body, giving some structure to the dead mess. Can't lift him otherwise, just a bag of bones.

Maria grabs his legs.

We lift.

We walk.

We trudge.

An old streetlight hangs limp and low in the sky, casting our collective shadow as something sickly pale, amorphous, shambling.

Someone in the pressing mob chambers a round in a gun. We freeze. I nearly drop the guy, grab Maria by the collar, and drag her off, melting into the mob. Problem is we won't melt, not with our white shirts. Not at four in the morning. Not here. Not now. All eyes are on us, and there're plenty. A fucking carnival. Day of the Dead. And if this dead bastard's someone's son, someone's brother? Oh, Jesus, if he's from a rival gang...

"Whose ground is this?" I hiss, looking around.

"Borderland ... disputed ... I think," Maria grunts.

The New Guard

"Hey … move it," I call out, hoping against all hope I part this venom-sea like Moses on his best day. But I don't. The sea doesn't move. Nothing moves. They press in harder. Leering. Talking. Someone shoves me, staggers me. Maria swears, but we both stay up.

An engine revs suddenly, followed by tires skidding to a stop. We're all a herd of gazelles at the water hole hearing a lion's roar. Everyone stops, everyone turns, everyone looks, everyone. Another set of bright spinning lights blaring injects me with a shiver of hope. The cops? Maria and I, together, stand bent, poised, craning our necks, looking, the hope welling inside our bellies destined for stillbirth an instant later.

"Cops?" Maria strains, looking.

We can't see shit through the crowd. We're too low, too bent. It's too thick.

"Cops? Here?" I ask, incredulous, spearing her and my own hopes in that instant, that instant of adrenaline induced pristine clarity that strips away all the bullshit choices and chatter, revealing what we both know deep down. It's not the cops. The cops don't come to this side of town. Not if they want to live. And besides that, we don't want the cops here, cause if they were, we'd be standing, dead to rights in the middle of a gunfight.

"Be cool," I say to Maria, but really to myself, cause I'm on the verge.

Heads peek back, over our shoulders, pressing in close, pressing in tight, asking questions, jostling us, bumping us, and it's too tight to move, too tight to breathe. I'm nearly shitting myself as I make out the tattoos scrawled across the wall of suffocating brown flesh.

"Shit," Maria hisses, her eyes going wide. She sees them, too. Reads them. The tattoos. And all of them are of eagles. Feathered wings spread across chest and back. Birds of prey. Blood eagles. Hooked beaks. Burning eyes. Scaled legs run down to long black talons.

From behind me, one of the eagles lays a hand on my left shoulder, digging his talons in. I wince. He says something to me, but my ears begin to buzz and my peripheral vision goes wobbly numb the moment I feel the press of metal against my right cheek. I don't hear what he says. For the sliver of an instant the metal reminds me of my whiskey flask, smooth and shining, comforting cool. But something's different. Something's wrong. I feel the smooth barrel of the gun slide along my cheek. It's not that it's a gun; that's not what's wrong. I know it's a gun the moment it touches me.

The New Guard

It's that the gun metal's not cool. It's hot. Acrid stink singes my nostrils.

I don't hear what he says, but I know.

So I drop the dead guy in the dirt.

* * * *

"What's worse than bad?" I ask. We're almost there. Less than a mile or so, and Maria's finally talking.

"You wait and see." Maria nods to herself, gripping the steering wheel, black cancer shadows sliding across her pretty face, conforming to it as they go. "I always heard about him, y'know? Ambulance world's a small one. Especially here. And I know everybody. People move around. A lot. Coming and going. Hired. Fired. People always talking. And I heard about him. You probably heard it, too, right? Sketchy shit. Spooky shit. Urban legend shit. Everyone's got their superstitions. Well, maybe I ain't heard it all, but I've heard enough. And I always chalked it up to all the same old superstitious bullshit. But … I was wrong. Cause I seen it."

"Seen what?"

"The thing with the phone." She snaps her gum. "I seen him do it. More than once." She looks off, suddenly spaced. "Seen other shit, too."

"Yeah?"

"Yeah…" she says, but she doesn't elaborate. She just sits there, nearly squirming.

"So, how's he know?" I ask.

"Shit…" she shakes her head, smiling to herself, a cold smile, a smile devoid of any humor. "I don't know. Who'm I? Just some hood-rat escaped from the projects. I ain't nothing. But you…" She glances over. "What was your nickname at your last job?"

I tell her.

"Yeah." She nods. "That's right. And it's true. We all heard about you. Well, my man, that's why you're here. Why the old man takes your shit. You got the touch. And it ain't Midas'. Old man pays you double what he pays me. And I'm a shit-ton prettier, ain't I?" She raises a perfect eyebrow, daring me to disagree.

"You are that."

"You don't believe in God, do you, Raff?" Maria rolls on, rolling the crucifix chained round her neck between two fingers.

"I don't know." I shrug. "Not really…"

The New Guard

"So you don't believe in the devil, either?" She sucks her lower lip, head bobbing lightly to the tunes again.

"No."

"You believe in anything?"

"I stopped thinking about that stuff … long time ago."

"Well, the old man," Maria shakes her head slow, "he'll make you believe in something, I shit you not."

* * * *

The car that screeched to a stop is not the cops.

It's worse than the cops.

And in Mexico City worse than the cops takes some doing.

Dual parallels of burnt black rubber slide up beside my ambulance, terminating in a tricked-out low-rider, all gleaming chrome, flashing grim crimson ground lights, engine revving raw, roaring like a calibrated jaguar. Five gang-bangers just sitting in there, sitting low, just glaring at first, then suddenly they burst out, one clambering out the near window, the others out the far door. One launches himself sliding across the hood, smooth as an action hero. They all have guns. They're all jaguars, and they're all armed to the teeth, which means we should all be ducking, dodging, praying right about now.

They level their guns.

The eagles reciprocate.

The choking mire of humanity walling Maria and me in evaporates instantaneously, like magic, a blur of flailing arms and legs and bodies bolting for cover. We're at the beach, in the water, and someone just yelled, "Shark!" People are running. Ducking. Desperate, they're trampling old ladies, hurling kids out of their way, crushing each other against the fence. Humanity's finest hour.

Before a shot's fired, Maria's on the ground and dragging me right down there with her. She's fucking nuts. With one hand she's clutching her crucifix, praying, and with the other she's feeling for a carotid pulse on the dead guy. And here I'm just trying to shrink behind him, use him for a bullet stop.

The bangers are all yelling. Screaming. Both sides. It'd be comical if I were watching it on television. Ridiculous. Here it's not. They're threatening and posturing, jabbing the air with their steel. Throwing insults before bullets. All that macho bullshit? Maybe the ones that live will brag about it over shots or coke? They're all straddling some ephemeral line of boys trying to be men and men acting like boys. A bad combo. Circular logic. They're all young, but they're all old. Nothing older than a man with a gun aimed at his head. Bangers, it's their lifestyle, their deathstyle. Take your pick.

Teeth grinding, fingers in my ears and Maria praying next to me, it stops. It all stops. No shots are fired. Not one. Even the insults stop. I look up at the eagle that drew on me, held his piece to my head. Shit, he even looks like an eagle. A long hawk nose hooks down from his forehead, a long somber beak. His eyes are fierce, sharp, focused. He seems suddenly older than before, his weathered skin lined now with age. And there's something else about him. I blink. Try to focus. I realize vaguely he's not carrying a gun. Clutched in his fist now is a long ebony club, gleaming black obsidian teeth grinning up one side and down the other, death's black smile. A necklace of eagle feathers and striated, tendon-linked bone covers his chest like armor, rattling as he roars at the jaguars.

I peek up and see the tenement across the street is gone; everything I know is gone, replaced by a wide abyssal vista edged by Aztec pyramids. But they're different, too. They're not just the same series of stone tourist traps I see every day, not some dead old gray things wearing away by degrees. They're things alive in the night. Angry gods of Aztec-old, they sit squat and wide, painted the deepest crimson, flames flickering up their sides, long serpents of burning torch lining the long steps to their peaks, reaching up into the infinity of the black starry night.

Maria grips my arm, clamps on it like a bulldog, muttering prayers, her eyes squeezed shut. I take her hand. Squeeze it.

The jaguars, too, have changed. Do they notice? Spears and toothed clubs are in their hands, and they stand ready to charge up the hill into us. Only one thing stops them.

It's like a nightmare. Standing there, between the two groups, two armies now, of Aztec animal warriors, is the old man. I know it's the old man. I know it's him in a way I can't explain, but it is him. In my gut I know it. But it's also *not* him. Gone is the shock of white hair, the tan wrinkled face, stooped shoulders. Before me stands a wraith made flesh, god-strong, its hands raised like some high bestial priest, holding the two armies apart. An obsidian knife gleams in one hand. Loops of animal skin and feather adorn him. Torch flames flick shadow and light dancing liquidly across his face, his torso. His ribs press outward, skin so tight I fancy I can see his heart beating within his chest. Even his spine is outlined, in bas-relief, running from under the shadow of his ribcage, disappearing deep down inside his prominent pelvic bones. There is nothing now but smooth taut skin pulled across ridged bone.

The New Guard

His face is skull.

He's talking, a sallow dead drone, hypnotizing, speaking some language I know I should know, but don't. But the two armies do. And they respond. Screaming eagles, all around, descend upon us with piercing war cries. Strong hands, predator claws pierce clutching onto my arms and legs, wrists and ankles, tearing me up from the ground. Cold stars glare down at me light years afar. I kick and flail, screaming, trying to hold onto Maria's hand, but can't. We're drawn apart, borne down the hill in a procession, the dead guy leading, me next, then Maria, down to the old man. Before a heavy slab of ancient stone, he stands, eyes glistening gold, twin pupils in each eye connected by an umbilicus of black. Atop a mound of bones he watches with those horrible eyes, waiting.

I know in that instant that Maria and I are truly going to die. As one, the eagles hurl the dead guy upon the altar. The jaguars have lined up behind the old man, offering some sort of salute with their obsidian axes and swords raised to their fallen brother. Whispering, hissing, the old man wilts down over the dead guy like a dying flower, covering him, soft, gentle, stroking his hair back smooth, caressing his face. Whispering. Their faces press as close as two lovers. The obsidian blade flashes, multifaceted, edge sharper than steel. He's cutting now, ripping a ragged trench. The dead guy doesn't move. In under the ribcage then, like slipping his hand into an obscene leather puppet, the old man's arm disappears to his elbow.

From the heavy stone slab the dead guy lurches up, eyes wide open, electrified alive, mouth gaping, screaming, screaming, screaming. The dead guy's hands scramble ineffectually at the old man's arm, elbow deep inside his defiled flesh. Horrified, I watch. The eagle warriors bear me toward the altar. I can't not watch. Slick and viscous, the old man pulls his arm free, a sucking rasp, ripping something from the dead guy's chest, and I realize dimly it's not the dead guy that's screaming. It's the thing being pulled out of him, the thing being taken from him, that's screaming. I shut my eyes, finally, trying to ignore the sound. I realize I can't. I realize it's too loud, too shrill, too unearthly, and I realize I can't distinguish it from my own as they hurl me onto the heavy stone slab.

* * * *

I awaken, clutched in someone's arms. That someone strokes my hair, whispers in my ear, holds me, comforting me with sounds, not words, amidst eruptions of her own misery. Maria. I can see the whites of her eyes, haunted in our darkness. Streetlights roll by and recede back into darkness in waves, one after the other, never ending.

"He had a pulse…" she whispers, maybe to me.

Another light passes by.

We're in our ambulance, the back. The dead guy's on the stretcher, lying full out, limbs flailed haphazard, looking all gray and diminished the way the truly dead do. Maria smoothes my hair, sniffs, praying, wipes her nose with the back of her sleeve. Her right hand still clutches the crucifix chained around her neck. Dried blood cakes her balled fist.

I wipe my eyes and look into hers. She's crying, too, black lines of mascara scarring her face horrid as she tries to hold it all back and fails. I can barely move, can only manage a whimper. I cup her cheek with my palm and she reciprocates, pressing her forehead against mine. She's quivering. I'm shaking. We sit there, holding one another, crying.

"A black night for my Black Cloud," says a voice.

Maria moves, but only her eyes.

I struggle, turning, look up front, see the old man driving. He adjusts the rear-view mirror, and I can see his eyes in the thin slit of gleaming chrome, those terrible eyes, pupils like binary black holes, locked on me, studying me. Looking away, I see them still, burnt into my vision like the residual afterimage of a lightning strike.

Steeling myself, I wipe my eyes, struggling to sit up, using the dead guy for leverage. Maria grabs my shoulders with both hands, pulls me back. "No..." she whispers. I look down at her crucifix, dangling there on a thin chain against her breast, nothing but a piece of gold, bent and twisted and broken.

"Who the fuck are you?" I yell up front.

In silence the old man stares at me through the mirror, considering...

"The old guard," he says with firm finality.

"And what the fuck's the old guard?" I demand.

"The old guard is the new guard," he says, those eyes turning back to the road, pyramids coming on, rising up fast.

Growling at Quarks

By William Sauer

"DARK MATTER."

"Dark matter? What's that mean, like there's still 30 year-old coffee in the coffee can?"

"No, I mean that there is dark matter in the coffee can."

"Like quarks and neutrinos and science stuff like that?"

"Yes, astrophysics. Particle theories. Dark matter."

"Why do you have dark matter in an old coffee can on a shelf in your storeroom?"

"Because I didn't know what else to do with it."

"You are absolutely killing me, Francis John. Where did you find dark matter, and how did you get it into a coffee can?"

"In the alley behind the shop, and I scooped it up like catching fireflies. I didn't want it expanding all willy-nilly and messing up the neighborhood."

"And how, pray tell, did you know it is dark matter?"

Growling at Quarks

"You sure are being nosy, Hannah. I don't know for sure, but I don't know what else it could be. I'm an antiques dealer, not a scientist."

"Can I look at it?"

"No way. It's been there for 17 years, and there's no telling how big it got."

"You do realize you're crazy, right? Whatever it is, it sure has Mosi worked up — Mosi, stop growling at Uncle Frank's quarks!"

* * * *

I loved my brother Frank very much, despite his eccentricities; probably more because of them. He owned a little antiques shop at the north end of Arkham, just outside Miskatonic University. That day I'd paid him a surprise visit to introduce him to Mosi Tatupu, my new shiba inu puppy.

Of course, I forgot all about Frank's coffee can of dark matter. Seven years later, he passed away. He never married or had children, so he left the shop to me. The day he died, I found myself back in the shop with Mosi, trying to clear my head before making arrangements with the undertaker. Mosi made a beeline for the storeroom door the moment we entered, growling with his nose to the threshold as if he could find a way under.

"What is it Mosi, is someone back there? Do you smell a mouse?"

Then it clicked. Without opening the door, I flicked on the light switch next to it and peered through the window. There it was, in the same spot it had been seven years before, the last time Mosi had been in the shop, and I had been in that back room. I shut the light off and kneeled to pat Mosi's back.

"Come on, Mosi," I said. "We'll have plenty of time for growling at quarks another day."

* * * *

Two years prior to inheriting the shop, my husband had left me for a twentyish MLC girl. My poetic justice came in the form of a lump settlement large enough to allow me to retire at 51, and I got to keep Mosi Tatupu. With my kids grown and overly sympathetic to their father's wallet, I decided to move from Boston to Arkham and keep Frank's shop going. Three weeks after the funeral, Mosi and I found ourselves back there, intent on cleaning up six weeks' worth of dust.

On cue, Mosi tried scratching his way under the storeroom door.

83

Growling at Quarks

"Once and for freakin' all," I cursed to myself. I grabbed a thick pair of welder's gloves from the inventory and headed to the back room. Mosi went straight for the shelf and sat at its base, looking up to the can on the second-highest shelf and growling with teeth bared.

"Mosi," I said, "it's just an old coffee can. Scootch!" He moved aside, just barely, as I stepped in while pulling on the second glove. "But I guess I can't be too careful, huh? Who knows what your crazy uncle Frank really did put in there?"

The can weighed more than I'd expected, as if full of lead shot. The best I could do was ease it down to a lower shelf for more comfortable examination. The 24 year-old duct tape sealing the black plastic lid closed had welded onto itself, so I had to find a utility knife. After carefully slicing all the way around, I lifted the edge of the cap ever so slightly.

The stuff that began to leak out resembled jet-black fog filled with a billion itty-bitty fireflies. Before I could reseal it, the top flew off with a pop and the sparkly black smoke flowed out over the rim. It didn't dissipate like fog or smoke would, didn't flow like liquid, didn't ooze like goopy pudding; it just roiled and flowed and spread out.

In a panic, I looked around the room while Mosi paced back and forth, barking his high-pitched *"hurry hurry"* bark.

All the while, he never went closer than eight or ten feet to the shelf. A thirty year-old green plastic turtle-shaped sandbox caught my eye, leaning against a wall and partially obscured by an armoire in need of refurbishing. I grabbed it, tossed the cover aside and set it on the floor at the base of the shelves. I tipped the can forward; the sparkly stuff floated down and began to pool in the bottom of the sandbox. Mosi finally stopped barking and sat several feet away, never taking his eyes off the oversized plastic turtle. It seemed to take an eternity, but the can eventually emptied, and the sandbox filled with Frank's dark matter.

While the transition happened, I sat cross-legged on the floor next to Mosi; I couldn't turn away either. As it spread out, the stuff in the turtle's back swirled and glimmered, some areas growing denser with changing colors taking on a cloudy, wispy look while other areas simply twinkled like a starry night sky.

"Mosi, doesn't that spot look like those NASA pictures of a nebula?" I asked, scratching his ears. "And the swirly bit looks like the pictures of the Milky Way."

Mosi just cocked his head. By the time the stuff had finished flowing, it looked like a tiny universe on the back of a giant turtle.

"Dark matter, indeed," I said.

Growling at Quarks

Mosi stood and cautiously walked over to the edge. Before I could get up to stop him, he gently pawed at one of the rainbow-colored clouds, tearing a black gash through it. He drew back and sat again while the spot he had created grew darker than the deepest pitch in any other area of the sandbox. The colors around it began collapsing inward, like sand sliding into a pit. Soon, only a three-inch black hole remained, surrounded by sparse twinkles for another inch or two. The rest of my little universe remained intact.

"I don't think you should do that again, Mosi," I said. Mosi stood again and sauntered off to the front room where he laid down for a nap.

The logical impossibility of staring down at an entire galaxy struck me as funny. The idea made me smile, my smile breaking loose into uninhibited laughter. I couldn't help but recall the Iroquois creation story of North America built on the back of a mighty turtle to save a fallen sky woman from sinking to the bottom of the endless sea.

* * * *

The descent began with an old rocking chair taken from the "to be restored" corner of the storeroom. As I sat staring into the Turtleverse, a thought came to me. What if there were teeny-tiny little planets in there, full of teeny-tiny life? Mosi's black hole could have wiped out millions, billions. I had to try and prevent it from happening again. If Mosi's gentle paw swipe could do that, I couldn't imagine the devastation if something fell into it, or if it were jostled or worse, moved. I appointed myself guardian of the Turtleverse, sky mother, protector goddess.

That removed all possibility of telling anyone about it. Even if they believed me and didn't lock me away for my own good, I couldn't envision any scenario that didn't end with so-called government scientists barging in and taking it, and me, away. A plan began to formulate as I lost myself in that sparkly black soup.

Frank had a part-time shop manager named Marlene. She ran things while he went off on what he called his "picking odysseys," his road trips to find stock for the store. She leapt at my offer to have her run the place full-time. She never questioned my rule that the back room would always stay locked, the only key being mine. I blacked out the window in the door of my new office and covered the windows facing the back alley with that solar-shielding vinyl that's so hard to see through. I rented a storage garage nearby to make up for the lost space. Every night for two weeks, I dragged everything from the back room to the front of the store so

Growling at Quarks

Marlene could have it moved out during the day. All that remained were the Turtleverse, my rocking chair, a small table and a mat for Mosi. He chose to spend most of his days out front with Marlene, but every now and then he would scratch at the door to come nap by my side.

My days were spent observing, taking notes and making sketches. Eventually, I found myself talking to whoever might be in there. Mostly random thoughts at first, then I started offering advice based on the story of my life, which I offered up almost in its entirety. The Turtleverse swirled and twinkled, but never offered anything in return beyond its inherent beauty. I needed more, so in an effort to paint my reclusiveness as eccentric, not crazy, I took up working with watercolors.

Marlene turned out to be a wonder. The shop flourished under her watch. She developed relationships with an entire network of professional pickers to keep stock rotating in and out quickly. After I accidentally left one of my paintings on the front counter overnight and talked my way out of explaining its inspiration, she labeled my work "galaxyscapes" and convinced me to let her sell them. They sold like mad. My store, my work, my life all blossomed without me.

William Sauer

There's a futon in the corner of the room now, and a kitchen island with a little fridge and an electric skillet. I even brought the armoire back for some clothes. I let Marlene move into my condo; her rent is the care and feeding of Mosi. They adore each other. It rains a lot in Arkham, so I sneak out into the back alley on rainy nights and let myself get drenched clean. Marlene brings me groceries and art supplies and takes care of my laundry. She doesn't question my quirks. I'm Frank's sister, after all, and she spent 15 years growing accustomed to his. Besides, never in her life has she done so well financially.

I've begun to wonder whether there really is any sentient life in the Turtleverse. If so, are they even listening to me, or are they raising their fists to the sky, screaming defiance at the divine voice lecturing them but doing nothing for them? Ungrateful bastards. Don't they know what I've given up to keep them safe, to watch over them? It's just so stressful. I've noticed that the Turtleverse never stops expanding, as well. That first day, it covered the bottom inch of the sandbox. Three years later, it was only an inch away from overflowing. I don't know where the dark matter came from, or why it became the Turtleverse, or why it's become my burden to bear. There is only one thing I know for certain: being a goddess is a lonely task.

Growling at Quarks

* * * *

My little Turtleverse overflowed on a Tuesday morning. Apparently, green plastic is not very effective as a wall of forever. There were no sparkles in the portion on the floor, so I decided to touch it. Dark matter is so weird. It rolls and flows like fog or smoke, but if I touch it, it's cold and rubbery like poking my finger into a block of tofu. If I try to grasp it, it flows through my fingers like water, leaving dense black drops behind for just a moment before it all joins back together. It is a gas, a liquid and a solid, all at once. It terrifies me.

By the next morning, the turtle pool became completely obscured by a blanket of sparkling black, rising up from the center and sloping down to the floor in a circle about a foot larger than the pool's circumference. I had to move my chair back to keep my feet out of it. Expansion is accelerating rapidly. Every day I have to move everything back farther. I'm almost to the wall, next to my futon. I can't change clothes anymore because the armoire is too heavy, and I'm too frightened to walk through the Turtleverse, too frightened I'll destroy galaxies and kill billions.

Even worse, it will keep getting deeper now. I've stuffed rags and things under both doors to keep it from escaping the room. I can only hope wood and glass and plaster can contain it. Now I can't leave; I just can't let it out. When there is no floor left, I will lie on my futon and wait for my destiny to rise up and take me. I imagine the whole back room filled floor to ceiling with my little Turtleverse. I imagine being engulfed by it, becoming one with it, one with all of my children. Then I will truly be a goddess.

Be Nice

By Gary Bonn

THE FUMES OF DIESEL THICKEN THE AIR. Huge dogs tethered in shadows watch and menace. Muddy paths have formed where grass used to be. Cables criss-cross, half trodden into the dirt.

Why do I notice these things first? Why not the flashing lights, the shrieks of joy, the roar of machinery, the smells of candyfloss and fried onion?

I'm an optimist; I *think* I am. I'm a good person, too, and try to be nice to people. But ... I don't have to look too far inside myself to touch the rage. I don't know if everyone has it; it's not the sort of thing people speak about.

It taints the way I see things. Like I should be looking at the sexy woman serving burgers, but instead I concentrate on the two men walking towards her. There's something in their speed and hunched body-language. Violence? Evil intention? It's hard to say, but it's not pleasant. I really don't know why people have to be nasty to each other. It demeans them and upsets me. It's really simple; all the prophets, philosophers, and profound people were right: just wise up, share, be considerate, and the world is a better place.

I'm also a bit of a wimp and inclined to panic; so when I find myself running towards the two men as they punch and kick the woman, I'm truly stunned.

So is the first bloke I connect with as I jump high and ram two feet in his back. Landing, I'm ready to launch myself at the other. He looks at me for a split second, and the woman gets one hell of a kick in. That's two big men down.

The first is struggling to rise; there's still fight in him, and I'm shocked at my ferocity as I stamp on his jaw. I know where my anger came from, two big blokes against a small woman. That sort of thing just shouldn't happen, but even so I think I overdid it with my foot.

Parents hurry their children from the scene. Some people just stare; maybe it's entertainment.

The two attackers scrabble away. They won't be back in a hurry.

"You alright?" the woman asks me. She's relaxed, like this sort of thing happens all the time. Close up, she's even sexier. Tight leather, from neck to toe, shows every curve, even the crests of her pelvis.

"Yeah ... yeah. Fine, thanks. You OK?" I answer.

She tightens the band holding her ponytail. "Thanks, mister knight in shining armour. That could have been a bad moment for me." She grins. "I'm Judy, and you?"

I shrug. "Jarno."

"Great name. I think I owe you a burger, Jarno. Onions?"

"Uh ... yeah, thanks. You don't have to."

"You didn't have to help me..."

"Why did they attack you?"

"Don't know. Salsa, chilli, hot chilli ... or, my speciality, demon sauce?"

"I dunno; you choose."

Her eyes sparkle with laughter; she tosses her ponytail and does a circular movement of her shoulder. I think she means it to be seductive. It's not, but what the hell? It's the fact that she meant it that works for me.

She says, "Demon sauce it is. Try it. If you don't like it, I'll give you another with something milder in." She assembles the burger in a blur of practised fingers. "Here." She wraps it in paper and hands it to me.

I take what I hope looks like a manly bite — the sauce is stunning. "Actually, that's awesome! Really good. You make that yourself?"

Be Nice

"Of course, but no one ever said anything so nice about it. Maybe it's an extra good batch." She holds her hand out. "Can I take a bite?"

I pass it to her. "Sure."

Her eyes close as she samples it and moans with sensual pleasure. "Wow!" She says and hands the burger back, her fingers lingering against mine.

This time I take a huge bite — and scream. Fire burns my mouth and throat, even into the salivary glands at the corners of my jaw. She's added something — something infernal from her own mouth.

I'm staggering, lurching, crashing against a caravan. Snarling, a Doberman launches at me only to be stopped by its leash.

People look away like they're seeing someone blind drunk.

God knows where I am now, or how long I've been stumbling around. I must be on the other side of the fairground. The burning has settled a bit and a bottle of icy water helps. I'm shaking; the cold plastic is nice against my sweating forehead.

What on earth did that woman do? That wasn't chilli, more like acid, but my tongue and mouth don't seem damaged.

The heat hasn't faded so much as passed into my body. It flickers and smoulders; not a bad feeling, just weird. I sit on a grassy bank in the dark. Dew soaks into my jeans. Below me, the fairground people pack up for the night. The noise fades; dogs are freed from their tethers and walked; lights go off, and quiet settles over the scene.

Time to return to my bedsit and another night of lonely boredom. A shortcut takes me through trees and bushes, along the back of the station and into the waste-ground by the industrial estate. I didn't expect people to be up and about — this place is deserted at night. Car doors slam and people crash through the undergrowth.

Someone runs towards me, twigs snapping and tearing at clothes. A woman carrying a screaming baby, illuminated by the distant motorway lights, emerges from shadow. She's terrified, panting, sweating, looking all around like someone's after her.

I feel the same surge of anger I felt when the men attacked the woman at the fair. Mothers and babies shouldn't have to run in terror; it's not right.

She stops when she sees me, hunches over, looks to the sides to see if there's another footpath to run down, but

Be Nice

there are only thorny bushes. I raise a hand and smile. It doesn't calm her. I step aside and motion her past me. She runs, sweat trickling down her neck. Her dress whips me as she dashes past.

People in pursuit. Men. There's noise everywhere, people shouting and forcing their way amongst the scrub. Two figures storm up the path towards me.

Now what the hell am I going to do? A lifetime's training in no-hope and failure, of being bullied at school and ignored thereafter has not prepared me for this moment.

But instead of the cold, emptying terror that is my usual response to danger, the fury mingles with the heat inside me. I feel strong, calm, and dangerous.

The figures slow and glare at me. "Who are you?" The speaker doesn't wait for an answer but looks back to the other. "Take him. I'll get the woman."

I'm not a fighter and don't know what to do. That thing at the fairground was dead lucky. If one of those blokes had hit me, I'd still be whimpering and daydreaming about what should have happened instead — anything that led to me winning and being heroic.

The first man dashes towards me, and I raise a hand to protect myself. Still three metres away, he stops, jerks like he's run into a glass door, staggers back and bumps into the bloke behind. They look around, hunched, confused, trying to work out what just happened. The leader gathers himself up and launches at me again. This time I raise my hand and make a pushing motion. Old leaves and twigs fly up from a shockwave that hits both of them, crashing one against a tree and the other through a bush and onto some crumpled corrugated iron.

Both men lie still; leaves and other debris settle as the vibrations of the iron fades.

More shouts. I think the noise attracted people. A tall black bloke pushes branches aside, steps on to the path, sees the two men lying and looks at me. His hand whips under his jacket and pulls out a knife.

I feel no fear, just an incredible calm. There's a force inside me, *and outside*; I can shape it, move it.

The black bloke approaches, poised to attack or run, eyes narrowed and flicking glances from side to side.

I stand, weight on one foot, hands in pockets. Not a threatening stance, but the man looks fearful. I think my lack of concern worries him.

"Who are you? What are you doing here?" he growls. Turning slightly, he shouts, "Boys! Over here."

More movement in the darkness, people swearing and stumbling in the poor light.

Be Nice

Behind the man, a woman screams. That's it; I've had enough of people being hurt by others; it's got to stop. I walk forward. The bloke tenses, and when I'm in reach, launches his whole body-weight behind the point of the knife. He may as well have tried to stab concrete. The blade snaps against my T shirt, and he bounces off me sideways, tripping and crashing into thistles.

I walk towards the screams. Without looking back, I feel the man rise and run towards me. A simple thought blasts him up, back, and wraps him among branches in one of the taller trees. God knows how he's going to get down; I don't think he has enough working limbs left to do it.

I leave the path and stride onto an apron of concrete. Two men and a woman work at the rear of an articulated lorry. As I approach, I can see they're struggling with a boy. Maybe they want to put him in the back?

Feisty little bugger, he's putting up quite a fight and shouting, "MUM!" A savage punch to the side of his face silences him and he sags, wailing. The woman's arm rises to strike again — and comes off, spinning through the air.

Maybe that was a bit cruel, but if that's the sort of thing she uses her arm for, then she's better off without it.

It takes her and the two men a moment to work out what happened. They drop the boy and look around, see me approaching. The woman staggers, clutches her useless shoulder. Blood pumps over the concrete.

Raising my hands I gesture as if pulling the container's doors further open. Metal screeches and explodes, and the two doors crash down onto the men. Pebbles and bolts bounce over the ground. Inside the lorry, huddled figures, men, women, and children, bound and gagged, stare out in horror.

Leaping up, I kneel by the first group and tear at their bonds. Cable ties, hard and narrow, gods that must be sore on wrists. How can people treat others like this?

After freeing them all, I ease myself through the crowded container. People rub sore limbs, hug children and each other, look at me with thanks and fear in their expressions.

I jump out and head home, only to see another man leap out of a car and run towards me. He's carrying something small. I think it's a pistol. Or machine pistol. Shit, I've really had enough of this. If I ruled the world, things like that wouldn't even be made.

He raises it, points it at me and shouts something. I can't even be bothered to listen. The gun drops; his clothes shred and fly in twisting ribbons. Stark naked, he rises, limbs flailing, into the night. I leave him tangled in a group of four power cables between pylons. If he survives, he'll have a nice story for the police and rescue services.

A car, hidden in shadow, starts up and accelerates away. Black, with tinted windows, I think it contains people who realise they're outclassed and want to escape. It's no big deal for me to bring a wall down and cover them in a thick heap of rubble. At least I didn't kill them; I think restraint is in order when you know you're winning.

No further incidents, well, until I get to the block of bedsits and flats.

Burger Girl leans at the entrance. She's smoking a cigar. Street lights glint off the shiny, tight leather that suits her so well.

She sees me and throws the cigar down, drops to her knees facing me and says, "My lord."

Well, bugger me. None of this was in my horoscope this morning.

"What?" I ask.

She looks up. "May I rise, my lord?"

"Stand up and stop pissing around."

She rescues her cigar, rises, leans against the doorframe again and takes a puff.

I ask, "What was your name again? Sorry if that seems rude, but it's been a weird evening."

"Call me Judy, my lord."

"And I'm Jarno, not your lord. What did you do to that burger?"

"I added a little sauce ... Jarno."

"Spit?"

"Sort of. Normally it just makes people sick — they tend to return and complain, sometimes violently. But I knew one day it would enter the right man and bring my lord and master back."

Maybe if she'd given me one piece of information at a time, I wouldn't be standing here with my mouth opening and closing.

She pushes herself from the wall and nods to the accommodation block. "You don't need to go back to that dump. I'll find something better for you." She reaches out. "It would be an honour to take your arm and walk with you."

"Fine." I run through the inventory of things I'm leaving behind. Clothes, most of them dirty and all of them old, a toothbrush... It's rather pathetic how little I possess. The only thing I'm going to miss is my collection of porn, but with a sexy woman that calls me my lord, maybe that won't be such an issue.

Be Nice

I'm glad to hear the strident sound of sirens converging on the industrial estate. Professional people will sort out the mess, take over where I left off, put the bad people in prison and look after the others. Maybe that was some human trafficking thing. I'm glad it's all getting sorted.

Judy has an arm around mine. She rests her head on my shoulder as we walk. "It's so good to have you back, my lord. I've felt so vulnerable without you and your strength. Did becoming a human give you the insight you wanted — the purpose you were looking for?"

Good question — if I knew what she's on about. I think hard, but don't answer. I don't want to give away the fact that I have no idea what's going on. We walk into the centre of town, all bright lights and groups of people sitting round tables outside all-night cafés.

I'm so hungry. The very thought of food sends my salivary glands to full throttle. My mouth waters, and I taste the fire Judy spat into my burger, but ten times more powerful. It doesn't hurt — I think I'm beyond being hurt. The fire spreads through me, lighting me up with energy.

Judy gasps, stops, looks up at me. "I can feel it... Power." She kneels again and rests her forehead against my knee. "I am your faithful and devoted servant." People stare, drinks or forks held halfway to their mouths.

"Get up, Judy. Let's get something to eat."

Again she looks up at me, wide pupils and eyes. "I will serve you," she says and marches into the nearest café. "Food! Bring it all, and we will choose." Turning, she asks, "Where would you sit, my master?" Her eyes are still wide, like I'm the most amazing thing she's ever seen.

"Anywhere. But can you quit the master, lord thing? I'm Jarno ... right?"

"As you wish." She turns back to the counter. "I asked for food…"

The sound of her voice, a cross between the hiss of a cobra and growl of a tiger, cuts through the room. Customers look away, look down, grab their coats and start to leave. Judy's voice is the sexiest thing I've ever heard — but these people don't seem to think so.

Any minute Judy will grow fangs and suck all the blood from my neck, or something. Nothing this good happens without an ending like that, but I could do with the free meal that looks like it'll come first.

I guide Judy to a table and pull a chair out for her. She looks to me and the chair, like she's amazed I'm doing something for her and not the other way around.

"What's going on, Judy? What's this all about?"

Be Nice

"You are my master, a man of great power. I am your servant. You lead; I follow. That's all there is to it." She looks at the nearest waiter and narrows her eyes.

"Judy, I don't think we should frighten people."

She turns back to me. "Is this a sign? You have a purpose?"

"Yeah, maybe." I sit too, and rest my chin on my hands. "I think there's too much evil in this world. I'd like to do something about it."

"Evil?"

"People hurting, frightening, abusing weaker people." I pause and look at her. "This power I have, how long will it last?"

"For all time."

A pale and hesitant waiter hovers near us. I turn and smile, hoping to put him at ease. It doesn't work. He looks like a rabbit asked to hand a petition to a family of foxes.

"Just bring lots of food ... something nice," I say.

Judy's lost in thought until plates are placed in front of us. Oh wow, I could live like this. I think that's real lobster. Don't know for sure — I've never had it.

As I dig in, Judy says, "That's brilliant, my lor ... Jarno. Too much evil about and you can stop it..." She shakes her head. "Amazing ... bloody amazing." Tears swell in the corners of her eyes. "Absolute genius."

"Hey, quit all that stuff and pass the ketchup."

"May I touch you?"

Hell, here it comes. I'm about to die horribly. "What?"

"Hold your hand?"

"Go ahead." I reach across and take hers. She gasps with delight and lays her other on top.

Tearing her gaze from my fingers, she asks, "What happened? Why all the police cars in the industrial estate? Was that you?"

"Yes, something to do with slaves and stuff, I think. Anyway, there were people hurting others, and I stopped it." I look deep into her eyes. "You helped me do that, Judy." I squeeze her hand. "Thank you."

A little gasp from her and she says, "My lord..."

"Jarno ... I give in. Call me what you will, but I do like Jarno."

"Jarno, there are many people in this town who suffer abuse."

"Well, let's get started after we've finished here."

She gives me that look again, like I'm offering her the world, and she can't believe it.

I think the waiters are glad to see us go. I mean really glad, like they're all going to head for the nearest church and pray thanks to God. It took me ages to get a bill out of them. Neither Judy nor me had enough money, so we said we'd pay when we could.

First stop, according to Judy, is a brothel under a posh hotel. I ask her how she knows it's there. She looks away and doesn't answer, but tells me the girls are slaves, some of them bought from distant countries. I never thought this sort of thing could happen in the UK. I can feel the fury rising in me. Judy hugs me tighter as we approach the place.

Posh hotel? It's like a palace! The whole façade is floodlit. Great sheets of glass — doors that open automatically for us. We stroll, arm-in-arm on deep carpets.

I put Judy under orders to be kind and friendly and not to scare the crap out of people at every opportunity.

The receptionist we're heading for may not know what's going on in the basements, so it's not fair to terrify her until we know she's in on it.

I don't know much about posh hotels, but I'm pretty scruffy at the best of times; it's after two a.m., and we have no luggage. Maybe that's why we don't get the huge corporate smile you see in TV ads. I mean, we could pass as rock musicians, but we failed to arrive in a Ferrari, or whatever they go around in.

The receptionist stands and says, "May I help you?"

It's difficult to know where to start this conversation. I let a ripple of power flit through my body, just to give me confidence that it's still there. Things could go horribly wrong.

"I believe there's a secret brothel of slave girls under this hotel, and I'm about to sort that out. Can you show me the way?" Not my best chat up line.

The woman's eyes widen. She reaches for a phone. I don't stop her; it's all part of her job. She only pushes one button, and the security guards come through a door.

"Before you say or do anything," I announce, "I'm going to see this through. Call the police, whatever, but don't try and stop me." I turn to Judy. "Check the ground floor and any stairs down. If we can't find anything, we'll have to take up the floors. In fact, it'll save time if we just do that."

The floor shakes. A vase falls from the desk and spills a load of fancy flowers. The carpet tears up, and boards snap, bursting up. The receptionist, all short skirt and long heels, scrambles over the desk. The guards help her towards the door. The whole place fills with dust; a siren goes off and there seems to be more noise outside. Under the floorboards, a layer of concrete erupts, and I wave all the debris across the front entrance. That should stop people entering and getting hurt.

Be Nice

Lights go out. Emergency lights, dim and spooky in all the dust, come on and illuminate a corridor and the corner of a room below. Judy and me climb down. I could probably jump, but I really don't know if I'd break something, or if I'm indestructible or what.

Judy presses switches; the lights work down here. I have to smash one locked door after another. All we see are stores and rooms full of ventilation equipment and stuff. Time to take up another floor.

I expose what looks like a living room below us. A man, cowering — hands held over his head, stares up, freezes at the sight of Judy and me, staggers back and tumbles over a sofa. He's dressed in a sharp, pinstriped suit.

This room is a lot higher, smooth walls and nothing to climb down. I grab Judy's hand, and we jump. Nice landing, no pain. Apart from the streams of dust trickling from the ceiling, this all looks quite luxurious, oil paintings and patterned wallpaper.

The man tries to run but struggles against the force of my mind. He can't possibly win such an uneven fight, but he struggles anyway — until I stand face-to-face with him.

"I'm not up for a conversation, or lies, or any crap," I announce. "You will bring everyone in here, everyone in this place. Or I will kill you. My friend will go with you to make sure you behave." I gesture to Judy.

The man doesn't move or say anything. He's a blank mask of confusion and terror. "Do you understand me?" I ask.

He nods, his eyes flicking up to the hole in the ceiling and back to me, as if still catching up with reality.

I say, "Do it then."

While they attend to that, I decide to go for a little exploration. Doors and corridors everywhere. I find I don't have to smash the locks; they do my bidding. Inside one room, a naked girl, with alabaster skin and blue, but otherwise oriental, eyes, lies on the floor, bound and gagged. Red weals and the bruises of strong fingers mar her skin. The bonds and gag burst apart, and I help her up and reach for what I suppose is her dressing gown.

"Who did this to you?" I ask, helping her cover herself.

She says something in a burst of Eastern speech that I can't understand. There's a glass and jug of water on the table beside the bed. I pour some and hand it to her. She takes the glass and gulps the contents, her eyes on me.

"Come on," I say. "You're safe now." Taking her arm, I lead her into the corridor. I'm stopped by the ghastly sight of a man, with an obscene mount of flesh, being forced out of another door. Struggling to pull his pants on, he looks in terror back into the room. I can only suppose Judy is in there.

I take a pace towards him. "Who are you?"

"None of your business."

"Oh, it really is. What are you doing here?"

"This," says Judy, leading a girl through the door. A thin teenager with ribs far too defined, like some anorexic. The girl looks frightened and follows Judy.

"Who the hell do you think you are?" roars Fat Man at me. "Get out of here."

"Nope."

"You've taken on far more than you can cope with…"

"No. You have," I reply. "But that's cool because I can help you with it. Does all that flabby gut get in the way when you mess with young women? I hate to think of it spoiling your fun."

"What…?"

A vertical stroke in the air of my finger and his abdomen opens from top to bottom. The entire contents erupt onto the carpet along with slabs of yellow fat. He sinks to his knees.

Pinstripes comes through the door, claps his hands over his ears as Fat Man screams.

Gary Bonn

Thin Girl throws up; Judy supports her as she retches. Oriental Girl strides forward, leans over Fat Man and rakes her nails across his eyes again and again. I don't stop her. I think he probably deserves it.

The commotion brings people tumbling into the corridor from rooms either side. Judy slaps Pinstripes and yells, "You're supposed to be leading them to the room. Get on with it."

So, she had to slap him. Interesting: she doesn't have my power.

Good.

I get the feeling two people with my talent could lead to World War Three.

Just before we get everyone into the big room, another man bursts from a bedroom and races for a wall. I suppose there's some sort of secret door there. He glances back at me and presses the wall. As it opens, I dislocate his femurs and break his wrists. I reckon that's all repairable; surgeons are really good these days. He's run enough, and people will need to speak to him. Good people that will put him and his kind in prison.

With everyone in the big room, I realise it's meant to sit far more. I ask Pinstripes why there are so many seats. He says something about more guests being accommodated at times.

Be Nice

There are twelve girls and young women here. Judy's looking after them. She's getting food from a trolley and drinks from a bar. I help carry and serve.

Judy stares at me like I'm the best person on earth and a source of profound wonder to her.

Pinstripes looks pale and scared. The slaves, mouths pulled half-open over clenched teeth and nails digging into the upholstery, look at him like they want to tear him apart. Maybe it will ease their pain if I let them?

I offer him a drink, and he says, "I'll see you dead first."

After his left eyeball explodes, I answer, "You won't see much at this rate. Are you going to learn that you don't mess with us, or would you like me to work on your internal organs?" He shuts up, apart from whimpering.

"I'm sure you have a family and friends. We'll find them. You resist me and they get punished. The police will come soon." I pass him a bar pad and pen. "Names and contact details of clients. Everything. Stop whining about your eye. Feel lucky that you still have another — for the moment."

I have to say, the police, SAS, or whatever, are really sneaky. Tossed through the hole I made in the ceiling, the gas grenades come as a surprise.

Nice to know we have people like this. I'm going to need them. For the moment, I'll just push the gas back up and rip the officers' masks off. "Keep writing, Pinstripes," I command.

Judy offers me a glass of Champagne, clinks her glass against mine, looks up into my eyes and says, "Wow!" She turns to the slaves and says, "Our Lord Jarno has freed you. You are all free to go. Some of you may return to your families and countries only to face humiliation and contempt. I, Judy, have an idea. I am Jarno's servant and follower. He has chosen to make war on those that cause suffering and abuse other people. The poor and the weak can turn to him for support; the rich and the cruel must cower. We need people in all countries; people who can help this cause — the final battle against evil. I can make you strong like me. Knives, bullets, and bombs will never harm you; no one can resist you once I've made you one of us. I can do this, but Lord Jarno can undo it and inflict pain and death if you stray from the cause. This is my promise. I will make you the new angels of good."

She smiles. "Sorry, long and scary speech. Anyone for another drink?"

Pinstripes is writing and whimpering still. I say to Judy, "I'll take another glass."

Be Nice

She grimaces and waves an empty bottle. "There's more, but it's not chilled. Shall we go upstairs?"

"Yeah, come on. It's a bit gloomy in here."

One of the girls talks and gesticulates to Oriental Girl, who looks from her to me to Judy in lightning fast glances. I assume there's some sort of translation going on.

Judy asks, "Lord Jarno, could you lead the way up? There may be some resistance, and these women are merely mortal. After all they've been through, it would be hard to see them suffer so soon after you rescued them."

Interesting. I don't trust her. This could be treachery, but she seems so sincere.

She must have seen my hesitation. She adds. "I could lead them up from that secret door. Could you go through the hole in the ceiling and make sure we'll not be attacked?"

Actually, that sounds even more like potential treachery. "No," I say. "It's best if you convert as many as possible now. I'll go up and have a look."

"Conversion takes time, as you know, but your wisdom is great. Thy will be done."

That sounds freaky, unsettling. I'm a bit embarrassed to admit that I don't really know what "Thy will be done" means. I walk under the hole in the ceiling and leap up.

I crash through a whole mass of cameras and microphones: didn't expect that. Bullets spatter off my skin and clothes. I don't fight back. These people will be on my side soon, and the world will benefit from their expertise. I just wait until the ammunition runs out or the people get bored of wasting it.

When silence falls, I say, "Gentlemen ... er, ladies — it's difficult to identify you under all that armour. I'm here in peace. I'm here to see that good is restored to the world."

I may as well be talking to bags of peanuts. The armoured figures pull back; others come forward. What I think may be rocket launchers point at me. Rocket launchers? That's one hell of a surprise. They must have already known about my power. How come?

"Stop this nonsense. You cannot kill me, but you can hurt or kill innocent people in the room below. So…"

I don't believe it. They're not listening. Fingers tighten on triggers. I flatten and bend the ends of the launchers. "I said stop." Just to add emphasis, I crumple every gun barrel in the place.

"You are about to leave and take everyone with you. There are some injured or dead people on the floor below. I, Jarno, am here. Take this message with you. Within one month from this very moment, all guns, tanks, missiles, and other weapons of war and anything to do with torture are banned throughout the world. The leader of any country in which these things remain, will suffer. That will leave a lot of countries without leaders. No problem — we'll supply replacements. Go now in peace, love, and kindness. The era of evil is over."

Well, that impressed no one. I suppose it's hard to listen to a prophet… Hang on; did I just think I'm a prophet? I'll put that to the back of my mind and return to it later. I may be out of my depth here — but who is really trained for *normal* life, let alone this weirdness happening to me?

The police or soldiers back away. This won't stop here. It'll be tanks or bombs next, maybe nuclear crap. Can I handle that? Yeah … I think so. Extending my senses, I can feel satellites in orbit, planes flying … nuclear subs deep underwater. I wonder if there are any limits to my power? That's scary. I only want to be an ordinary person who's nice to others. But there's that niggle; I'd like to be someone who convinces everyone that being kind is more important than anything else. When you know you can actually do that, how can you not act? If you see a child fall in the deep end of pool, and you're the only person that can swim — do you turn away and say that it's someone else's responsibility? I'm not that heartless.

Anyway, I told these people it's time they left. It's just a matter of putting some force down the corridors and pushing everybody out of whatever door or hole they came in by.

But that puts them out and leaves us in. I'll bet they don't give a shit about the slaves. It'll be bombs next. It's me they want.

I drop down into the big room again. Judy stands among twelve women staggering, clutching their throats and crashing into walls and furniture — the dance of the demon sauce. Pinstripes looks very dead. My eyebrows rise.

Judy shrugs, "He said he'd finished writing…"

I look at the corpse. Superficial injuries and massive blood loss — the slaves got to him. Whatever.

As I glance over the lurching and whimpering women, Judy says, "They're all up for it, all your disciples. They've taken my saliva." A grin from her. "Not burgers; I only had plastic-wrapped sandwiches." She looks down, hugs herself and twists into a sculpture of tension, walks over to me and curls at my feet. "Master, I couldn't make them less powerful than me. Please, may I be your head servant? I've waited so long, my lord, my lord." She clutches at my ankles and kisses the hem of my jeans.

No way. This is too much. I reckon this woman is more intelligent, cunning and downright evil than I could ever be.

Be Nice

I'm being set up for the biggest fall in history, but I can't help being pulled in. It's all so fascinating and heady. I don't even begin to hope that somehow I'll outsmart her in the end. It's going to be painful, humiliating, and I'll wish I had never met her; I'll torture myself for my own stupidity more than she can ever hurt me … *but*…

I pull her up. "Let's get them upstairs and somewhere more comfortable. I could do with another drink of cold, bubbly stuff."

* * * *

The hotel is completely empty except for us, well, after the last of the services scurry away. Judy says the slaves are invulnerable now — despite the agony her saliva still causes them. Will these people really be less powerful than me? I'm not sure: I'm not sure of so much. If I'm some sort of reincarnated lord, why don't I remember anything?

I look after the women, while Judy finds the kitchens. I stroke foreheads, wipe brows, squeeze hands, murmur words of comfort… The women are recovering.

My senses alert me. Here it comes; I feel two aircraft hurtling into the area. Their engines die as I smash the compressor blades; I'm pretty sure the pilots will eject and survive. It'll be missiles next, possibly within minutes. I suppose it depends on how many people have been evacuated, or how many civilians the authorities are prepared to kill. I'll stop the first missiles and any that follow, but I wonder what conversations are happening between the UK and other countries? "Yes, we are about to launch strategic missiles, but only to destroy a hotel in our own country, so don't worry. Have a nice day."

A clever thought. I may not be the brightest person, but I reckon the police will have stuffed this place full of listening devices, so I say, "Good evening, people of the world. All weapons aimed at this hotel will be redirected to Moscow and Washington. Thank you. That is all."

I'm worried about one girl. I reckon she's about seventeen. Olive skin, sharp features, probably European. There's no denying she's incredibly sexy, but she's shivering and sweaty. Something's not right. I slide beside her on the sofa of the main lounge and hold her in my arms. Can I heal people? OMG! *Can I?*

Apparently not; nothing happens. When Judy returns, pushing an overladen trolley, I say, "Judy, this one's sick, really sick. Can we get a doctor?"

Be Nice

"She's fine," Judy growls, like I'm about to fall in love with the poor girl and reject Judy forever. "Nothing can hurt her now … except you."

I release the girl and jump up. "Is it me? Am I making her sick?"

Judy softens and laughs. "My Lord Jarno. No, you are not making her sick. She's working though some serious disease, cancer, or something; she'll be fine."

She lifts food from the trolley, looks back at me, freezes and says, "What's wrong?"

"Missiles. Some from the Atlantic… Oh God, some from Europe, sodding *Europe*." It takes a moment for this to sink in. "People were expecting this, expecting us?"

"Yes, they were. It's all predicted in the Old Testament."

Missiles, crippled in mid-air, fall to the ground or into the sea — their engines and rockets failing. I crush components; propellant blazes into the skies. I only hope the warheads don't go off. The people who launched them will be safe in bunkers — it's the innocent that will suffer. The fury boils again.

Judy gasps and sighs. "The strength pours from you, my master." She kneels and, holding a glass of Champagne, offers it to me in both hands. "Of course they expected us.

Gary Bonn

They always expect something like us. If only they wouldn't. If only they would bloody grow up and not need someone to come and save them."

I'm expected to save the humanity? So, just when I'm getting my head round all these new developments, Judy goes and scrambles me again. No time to discuss it now. Some of the women have almost recovered. Soon we have to train these disciples and send them around the planet.

I think. I talk to Judy. I discuss with the twelve, but it's all useless. They only want my decision, my direction.

That's not hard. Bottom line: when the stronger hurt the weaker, the strong must be punished. Natural selection will see to it; evil will no longer promote survival. Evil is doomed.

* * * *

It's a pretty simple message and, when the twelve are ready to travel, they don't take long to spread it across the world. Some wander; before long others run countries.

It all goes well. Well, some countries and doctrines try to resist, but resistant people end up with the dodo and the dinosaurs.

I work out that evil is not just about intention to harm; there's an element of ignoring the suffering of others, the

Be Nice

starvation and poverty. Frankly, that's just as bad, in my mind. As a group we do warn people — once — to care for others. After that there's punishment. Hard, I know, bloody hard, but I think the world's moving away from greed.

I stay in the hotel; Judy's always flying round the world sorting things out. It's a bit of a lonely life for me then, but lovely when she returns, like now — all smiles and open arms. I fancy taking her back to that restaurant — and paying the waiters this time.

Skinny Girl phones me from Sri Lanka. "Master, hello."

"Hello, you. What's new?"

"Today I saw a woman beat her child. She was too violent."

"And?"

"I killed her."

"Don't feel bad. This is all leading to a new world. Love can be hard, so always keep the future in mind."

"I don't feel bad. Everyone knows we are doing good. You're saving the world, master; we all follow you."

"While I rule: there will be no evil."

Muse's Lament

By Patrick LeClerc

I WAS STUNNED WHEN HE CAST ME ASIDE. Shocked at how cavalierly I was replaced.

I thought I'd meant so much to him. He certainly acted like it. When we were alone he'd hold me close and whisper how much he needed me, how he couldn't let me go.

I know I gave him all I could. I was his inspiration, his confidant, the one he opened up to, the one he could cry in front of.

But now, looking back, I can see how it was all one sided. How he put me on a shelf when he didn't need me, only to reach for me again when things got tough. How he drained everything I had and left me hollow, empty. How I never got credit for the inspiration I gave him, only blame for his bad behavior.

I had just enough left to feel sorry for my replacement. Younger, unspoiled. To see the sparkle in his eye when he looked on so much he could take and savor, how much I had once had, before he took it. I knew how tenderly his fingers would caress those curves, how he would gently remove that top...

I'm only happy that I can't see it.

Down among the other empties in the recycling I'll never see him tip the new bottle into our favorite glass, the one he bought specially for me because it made me look so good, he'd said, or see the pain vanish from his face when he sips at the amber fluid, leaving it emptier each time, never giving back or giving credit.

It will all be over soon, I tell myself.

On Wednesday the trash man comes.

Turbulence

By Russell Jones

"...AND NOW THAT WE'VE REACHED OUR CRUISING ALTITUDE the seat belt sign has been turned off. Feel free to move around; stewardesses will be by to take drink orders shortly. Thanks for flying with us today."

James relaxed his grip on the armrests and breathed a sigh of relief. The passenger on his left tugged at his nose and pulled his earplugs out as everyone else on the flight settled into their routines. A fussy child a few rows ahead of him was handed a pair of headphones; an older man behind them pulled out a paperback, and James reached to retrieve the laptop he'd stowed under his seat.

It wasn't the first time he'd had to fly cross-country, but take offs never got any easier. The same weight pulling at his gut, the feeling his seat was going to tip him back and dump him into oblivion, never went away.

Turbulence

"Want some gum?" the man sitting next to him asked, holding out a plastic can.

His dislike of small talk never went away, either. James took the proffered gum and nodded, tossing it into his mouth before refocusing on his typing. He'd forgotten his earbuds in his luggage, but if he looked like he was busy enough...

"So, business or pleasure?" the man asked, a friendly smile stretching across his broad face.

Or not.

"Business," James said. "I'm in network solutions."

"Oh, so you go around and tell all the technophobes like me what we're doing wrong, right?" the man said, chuckling. He was wearing a striped collar shirt with suspenders, and had a battered briefcase on his lap.

James bit back a retort. "Sure. That's about right." He turned back to his typing.

"So what did the knuckleheads do this time?"

James sighed, closing his laptop. He wasn't getting out of this one. "A worm got into their database and corrupted everything. I'll have to help rebuild their server architecture, debug the network as a whole, and give a lecture on safe browsing practices."

The man whistled, rubbing a hand over his bald head. "Sounds like a tall order. Anybody I'd recognize?"

"You ever order pizza over the phone? Have to give them your credit card information?"

The man nodded.

"I'd consider checking your credit report."

The man laughed, a harsh barking that caused the older gentleman to look up from his book and scowl back at them in disapproval. James shifted uncomfortably.

"These computers ... it's always something, eh?" the bald man said, nudging James in the arm. He caught a strong whiff of body odor, like a forgotten gym sock left in a pair of shoes too long.

Someone forgot to put on deodorant, James thought.

"So how did the worm get in there? Some desk jockey go poking around a porno site?"

James squirmed in his seat and glanced around. A stewardess had a cart ahead of them and was talking to the mother with the fussy kid; it didn't look like they'd heard his overly loud seatmate.

"So how about you," James said, trying to change the topic, "what do you do?"

"Ah, now that is interesting," the man said. "I'm in sales and acquisition. Pretty big firm, but they like to keep us on a short leash, remind us who the real big shots are. I mean, look at me sitting back here in coach like some poor fucking soccer mom, right?"

James shifted again, trying to get as far into the aisle as he could. A few people turned and shot them dirty looks, but the stewardess and her clattering cart were still taking up most of the attention.

"Yeah, my boss knows I could sell shit to an asshole, but he still doesn't trust me to take on the big gigs. You know, get in bed with the big boys, find that nice tender spot and just fuck 'em 'til the money just comes and hits you in the face, you feel me?"

The man's stench was getting worse, body odor just rolling off him; James could see big pit stains forming under the guy's arms, and it was taking all he could not to gag. He wanted to get up, but the stewardess had moved to the people in front of him and blocked the aisle with her snack-laden cart. He'd have to get up when she moved past...

"In fact, that's why I made sure to get the seat next to you, mister James Robert Sandoval. Son of Roberto Horatio Sandoval and Vanessa Renee Peck Sandoval. Husband to Jessica Marie Sandoval, and father to precious Valerie and young Timothy."

James forgot all about the smell as his blood froze. He turned slowly back to the man, who had the same overly friendly, toothy grin on his wide mouth. It seemed to stretch past the corners of his chin and reach almost to his ears, the kind of predatory smile a cartoon cat would have as it eyed a bird it intended to eat.

"How ... how do you know all that?" James asked.

The man's smile stretched wider into something almost grotesque... James' cheeks hurt just looking at it ... and he patted the briefcase in his lap. "Oh, Jimmy James, Jim-bo," he said, "I know so much more than just that. It's rule one in sales: do your homework. Know the client. Know what they want, and what they'll do for it. That's why I'm here today, to make you the offer you won't refuse."

James' mind was racing as he tried to process what the man was saying. Was this some sort of con, some kind of scam run by a hacker? He could be a head-hunter, someone his company's competition hired to get him to leave his current job. It didn't makes sense, though; James was just a little fish, a consultant; there were easily a half dozen other people who would be more valuable in his department alone.

So ... why him, why here?

He cleared his throat. "Just what do you want to sell me?"

Turbulence

The man giggled as he cracked his knuckles. "This is my favorite part, you know. The looks on their faces, the questions, and then the rush from the answers. Their faces dawning with comprehension. Never gets old, you know? It's what gets me up in the morning, gets the coffee going, gets you through the long-ass commute; just to see that look, that *what-the-hell* look when I make an offer. I've snorted coke, a little crystal meth, even tried absinthe once ... not that fake shit, the real *wormwood and faeries in the bottle* deal ... and there's nothing like it in this existence."

James gritted his teeth. "Look, what the hell do you want from me?"

The man's grin faded, and his face grew serious. "You are going to die exactly a half-hour from now," he said, "and I want to sell you a way out of it."

James blinked. "That ... no way," he sputtered. "That's just stupid."

The man's face stayed serious. "It is true. In thirty minutes a bolt from the engine outside my window will work its way loose. It will cause the engine to flame out, and the explosion will tear this section of plane off. Your seat and the six around it will be sucked out of the fuselage in the aftermath and be found in a Wisconsin cow field. It will take three days for them to find all the parts of your body necessary to make a positive ID. The funeral will be closed casket. Your widow and children will wind up putting about a third of you into the ground while the rest of you will be fertilizer."

The blood drained out of James' face. Around them conversations continued like nothing unusual was happening; none of the people who'd shot them angry looks before seemed to be paying attention, and the stewardess was continuing to take orders just a few feet away.

"You're sick," James finally said.

The man leaned forward, and a fresh wave of stench washed over James. "No, I'm the guy who has your ticket out," he said with a hungry edge in his voice. "I'm not even asking that much for it. In fact, I bet you're going to like the transaction a lot more than you think."

"What can I get you gentlemen to drink?"

James twisted around, startled. The stewardess stood above him, bending over slightly so they could see her brassy nametag — *Cherry* — where it was jauntily pinned onto her blue-and-orange jacket. It also gave a pretty clear look down the front of her thin white camisole.

James felt the man ... *thing*, he suddenly thought ... behind him lean forward. "I'd like to have your legs on a plate," it said, its rancid breath hot on James' ear and neck, "with my face buried in them as I carve a hole in you so big you'd never be able to get filled to your satisfaction again.

Cherry smiled sweetly, then reached back and cracked open a can of ginger ale, pouring it into a plastic cup with ice. "And you, sir?" she said to James.

James stared at her. "N ... nothing," he said weakly.

"Well, I'll be back around if you change your mind or ya'll need a refill," she said. She leaned across to hand the drink to James' seatmate, and he felt her breast lightly brush his shoulder. She gave a little wave and pushed the cart to the next row.

James looked back at the bald creature sipping ginger ale next to the window. It looked back at him, its irises a solid, featureless black as they drank in his reaction. A drop of sweat rolled off the thing's nose and into the ginger ale, smoking and sizzling where it hit.

It's ... it's just not possible, he thought.

"Oh it's very possible," the thing said, smacking its lips. "In fact, it's a very little-known but still-documented fault in these engines. Best guess was something like this could only happen once in every million trips and only if the regular maintenance checks were ignored. Statistically it's so uncommon as to be effectively impossible, but you know what they say," it grinned its predatory grin again, "all it takes is once."

James couldn't breathe. It took a full minute for him to force his lungs to work again, during which his brain sprinted around in circles spouting gibberish. "You ... what are you?"

"I told you, Jimmy-James," it said patiently. "I'm the guy who can get you out of your predicament. The one with the plan. The man with the golden parachute. Figuratively speaking, of course, we're trying to avoid the whole *jumping out of the plane* thing."

"But ... you ... she didn't hear what you said, did she?"

The thing chuckled darkly. "You'd have to ask her what she heard. Which, incidentally, you'll get the chance to do once we finalize the details."

The briefcase latches snapped open of their own accord and the thing started rummaging around inside, pulling out a couple of manila folders and two pens. It unscrewed the cap on one to reveal a black, stone like nib which glittered like onyx, then started using it to scratch some notes onto one of the papers, filling in blanks with things like dates and locations.

"What do you mean? What details?"

"Oh you know," it said, "the foreswearance of all prior oaths and birth rights, standard acknowledgement of dominion, the payment schedule... It's a lot like those big walls of text you programmers always tell people to agree to before they can open their email or start playing their video games." It shot James another toothy, shark-like grin and went back to writing notes.

"But you ... wait a minute," James said, "this can't really be happening."

"Afraid so, J.R.," it said. "Gonna get this one in under the wire, but we'll get it done. You'll be back on your way to de-worming networks and telling the sheeple to stop clicking on titty pages in no time. With a little extra spring in your step, of course."

"What do you mean?"

"Ah, good, the denial's done, and he's ready to talk turkey," the thing said, putting its pen down. "It's quite simple, really. To complete this transaction, there needs to be a certain...

consummation ... to the agreement. Simply signing on the dotted line won't work; well, at least not with *this* pen," it giggled.

James frowned. "What are you getting at? What will this ... deal ... cost me?"

The thing grinned, then reached out and grabbed the collar of James' shirt; a thrill of terror shot through him as his ear was pulled next to its sweating, snarling lips.

"You're going into that bathroom back there, and you're going to fuck that stewardess until she forgets which way is up. You're going to plow her a row so deep and wide, she forgets her own name. You're going to send her screaming into what the frogs call 'the little death,' all while the rest of your fellow passengers are screaming their fucking heads off because the plane's suddenly forgotten how to fly."

James jerked out of the thing's grip. "What?! Are you insane?"

The thing kept grinning. "I told you it was a cherry of a deal," it said, then snickered. "Cherry ... that's pretty funny. I'll have to remember that when I get back to the office."

James hastily unbuckled his seat belt and threw his laptop into his shoulder bag. "That's it, I've had enough of this," he said as he stood up.

"Now hold on, Jimmy-legs," the thing said, reaching toward him.

"Get bent!" James said. He turned down the aisle to find another empty seat ... and was greeted with a wall of darkness. Two rows in each direction the seats just disappeared into a pitch blackness so deep James couldn't even make out the edges of the plane's cabin. It wasn't a

Turbulence

shadow so much as a ... *maw*. The more he looked at it, the darker it became, until he started to think he could see things *moving* in its depths...

A hand touched his shoulder. "Why don't you come sit back down?" said a calm voice behind him.

James jerked around, and saw the thing in the suspenders was now standing up. It had also transformed; its legs were shorter and thicker than a normal person's, stretching its brown polyester slacks to the point of almost ripping. Its fingers had lengthened into slender, talon-tipped protrusions, all sallow skin and bony knuckles. Its ears had also stretched into fleshy points, and its eyes were entirely black: two voids set back into its sweat-covered face and filled with the same deep darkness now surrounding James.

James stood a moment longer, then sank down into his seat; his arms trembled as he lowered himself back against the cushion.

The creature shuffled past him, sucking in its gut as it heaved itself over James' legs. The smell it was giving off had intensified from unwashed sweat into rotting eggs and stale urine. James felt bile rising in the back of his throat as the thing started straightening up its papers, clumsily pulling them together with its unnaturally long digits.

"Now," it said, "back to business. I've lined out all the terms in the agreement on this page, which you can initial here, and here, before signing this..."

"What did you do with the rest of the passengers?" James asked, staring at it.

"Oh, they're still here," it said. "We're just ... a little sideways right now. It's easier to do once in the air; you wouldn't *believe* how much trouble these negotiations can be on terra firma. This just ensures the parties are not disturbed, and the transaction is not aborted prematurely. Trust me," it said as it pointed at the walls of darkness, "you do *not* want to try to walk through that if you suddenly have go to the bathroom."

James shook his head. "This isn't happening. I'm just dreaming, or you slipped me something in that gum..."

"Now now, don't insult me," the thing snapped. "I would never act in bad faith like that."

"*Bad faith?*" James snarled. "You threatened to kill me, then told me to fuck some random stranger!"

"I did not, in point of fact, threaten your life," the creature said, raising one taloned finger. "I merely pulled the curtain back and shared with you information pertinent to these discussions which you were not aware of ahead of time. And as for Cherry..."

Turbulence

The creature snapped its clawed fingers, and the stewardess bounded up the aisle out of the blackness.

"Oh, are ya'll ready for that refill now?" she chirped as she twirled a lock of her strawberry blonde hair around one manicured figure.

The creature raised its talon again, and started humming. The stewardess flushed, and began breathing heavily as she slowly unbuttoned her jacket.

"What are you ... stop that," James said, both to the creature and the woman undressing in front of him.

Neither of them showed any sign that they heard him. Cherry ground her hips into an impromptu striptease, messing her hair with one hand as she tugged her camisole up over her head with the other. She removed the sheer silk, revealing two curves of flesh pressed together by a nude bra. Her legs buckled into a deep dip as her hands moved over the mounds on her chest, and she moaned as she leaned toward James.

"Did you know young Cherry here, or Charity as her mother named her, works part-time as an exotic dancer in between flights?" the creature whispered into James' ear. "She's taken her clothes off for a lot more men than yourself, and hasn't once felt an ounce of shame. I know for a fact she's had more than a few liaisons with other passengers ... and not all of them were men, either. 'Perks of the position,' she likes to brag to her friends."

Cherry leaned over, her hands on the armrest and breasts pressing toward James' face. He tried to pull back but was torn between avoiding the woman in front of him and touching ... whatever the thing was behind him. A lock of her hair tickled the side of James' face as she leaned forward; he tried to brush it away, just as he tried to ignore the uncomfortable pressure growing between his legs.

"Are you sure you don't want ... anything ... from me?" the half-naked stewardess breathed, biting her lip just inches away from James' face.

The creature snapped again, and Cherry was suddenly standing in the aisle, fully clothed, looking at James worriedly.

"I mean, you don't look too well," she said. "I could get you a water, maybe put a little seltzer in it. Would you like that?"

James shook his head, nodding quickly. "Yes, please," he said. "I want ... I would like a water, please."

Cherry flashed another dazzling smile and disappeared into the darkness toward the back of the cabin. James took three deep gulps of air, adjusting his belt as he sat back up.

Turbulence

"Now's your chance," the creature next to him said, waving a hand. The darkness pulled back, revealing Cherry striding down the aisle back to the bathroom and curtained stewards' area.

"What…" James whimpered. "I can't…"

"Oh, don't be a pussy, of course you can!" the thing said. "It's not like you haven't done this before."

"No, I haven't!" James protested. "I'm pretty sure I've never had to make a deal with a … whatever you are to screw some stripper so I don't wind up dead!"

The creature clucked its teeth. "That may be true," it said as it pulled out one of the manila envelopes, "but our records show in the past you needed a lot less convincing."

"What … what are those?" James asked as the creature started sorting through the papers in the folder.

"Oh, I think you referred to them as 'conquests' back in college," it said. "Let's start with freshmen year. Remember what you had to do to join that fraternity?"

It plunked down a college newspaper clipping. The headline read *SARAH CROWLEY WINS DEBATE AWARD* right above a black and white photo of a young girl with bright blonde hair, a beauty mark next to her eye and a slight weight problem.

"'The Chasing of the Chubbies', I think you all called it. The bigger they were, the quicker you stopped being a pledge."

"I … look, I didn't join them…"

"Not that semester, no … you didn't find out until after your little walk of shame just how much it cost to get in. But next semester, with a little extra scholarship money and three brand new letters on your chest, you were like a sailor on shore leave."

Three more photos were pulled out and plopped down: one of a girl in a cheerleader's uniform, another holding a flute, and a third posing for what looked like a magazine shoot in a skimpy bikini. "You juggled these three for two semesters before they caught on. Then came the twins," out was lain a photo of two blondes, identical except for a single set of braces, "whom you managed to keep in the dark for a full eight months."

"That was a misunderstanding," James said, "I had broken broke up with Trina long before I slept with Tracy."

"Yeah, 'long' meaning 24 hours and 'broken up' meaning you didn't return one phone call. Still didn't keep you from hopping into the sack with her, while her sister was out of town at a job interview. Three times."

Two more photos joined the row. "Don't forget Pamela, the freshmen you tutored, and Samantha, her roommate. I hear Pamela was devastated when she caught you giving her best friend a private session."

James shook his head as more photos piled on to the rest. The creature knew everything: the intimate details, the favored tactics, even the things he'd never told his wife about, like the two times he'd had to pay for morning-after pills.

"And of course," the creature said, "there was Jessica. The office romance. The crown jewel in your collection, the one whose friends congratulated for taming the wild stallion. The wedding, I understand, was beautiful."

A photo of men and women in formal attire and bare feet on a beach joined the rest.

"Of course, the bachelor party the night before was almost as epic." Another photo, this time from a cell phone camera, landed on top of it: the glassy-eyed girl next to James had bright blonde hair and a beauty mark next to her eye, and had obviously lost a lot of weight since her college days.

"I never knew Sarah was her cousin," James said. "But I didn't cheat on Jessica."

"No," the creature said, thoughtfully. "Not if you consider a little under-the-table blowjob for old time's sake 'cheating'. I guess that would be true, then."

James rubbed his hands over his face. "Look, what is the point of all this? I was a stupid kid in college. I met Jessica, things changed. That's not who I am anymore."

"Is that what helps you sleep at night?" the creature asked, propping its sweat-soaked chin up on one sallow hand. "Do you think to yourself, 'I work hard, I provide for my family. Doesn't matter that I never get laid anymore; I love my wife; I'm not that man. Who cares that I spend all my time neck-deep in some asshole's computer so my little rugrats can make it to college without bankrupting me? At least I'm faithful.'"

It leaned toward him, dripping sweat over the armrest and spotting James' khakis. "Quit bullshitting yourself," it said, stabbing a finger into his face. "Those women you banged are absolutely as much a part of who you are as is the name you were given. You climbed a mountain of pussy to get to where you are, and I for one think you should be congratulated for that." It fired off a mock salute which flung droplets of sweat all around the cabin and sent a fresh wave of rotten-egg-smell wafting past James.

"I worked hard to get where I am," he said, "and you're telling me I'm going to die in the next few minutes if I don't

Turbulence

throw it all away and go bang some stewardess, which is still something so absolutely insanely impossible that I can't even believe I'm considering it?"

The creature settled back into its seat. "Look at it this way, Jamesy-poo, what would your wife tell you to do if she were here?" It snapped its talons.

The woman two seats ahead of them suddenly turned around. She looked nothing like James' wife, but when she opened her mouth it was Jessica's voice which came out and sent a spear through his heart.

"Honey, what are you doing?" she asked in a perfect imitation of Jessica's irritated, tired voice. "We need you. I don't care what you have to do, but we need you to come back to us. You know I can't do this all on my own."

The woman's fussy child ducked into the aisle, pulling her headphones off. "Please, daddy," she said in a frightening copy of Valerie's whine. "I want to see you again. I want to show you the drawing I made of you at work." She held up a piece of airline stationary with a blue-and-red crayon box drawn on it; a stick figure stood inside with a wrench, smiling as it pounded the sides of its colorful prison.

"I know all about those other women," Jessica's voice said again through the stranger's mouth. "I knew about them when I married you, and I forgave you. I'll forgive you again. I just need you to make it home in one piece. I need you, James."

The creature pulled James back into his seat. "All you gotta do is sign here, initial here and here, and you're ready to dodge death and see that lovely family of yours again. After a quick trip to join the mile-high club, of course."

"But ... I just don't understand," he said weakly. "How does this save my life?"

"Aw, geez, do I have to spell everything out for you, Jimbo?" the creature sighed impatiently. "You go into the bathroom with Cherry-bomb, hike the knickers up and start the fireworks. You stay in there long enough and have such a good time that you don't even notice the seat you used to be in gets sucked out the window when the engine goes. You could ride her all the way down to the ground and nobody will even notice, because they'll be too busy *crashing*."

James shook his head, trying to think clearly. "What do you get out of all this?"

The creature spread its claws. "A steady paycheck, nice benefits, probably even a promotion after this gig. I tell you, you're quite the catch for me, and bringing this puppy in for a safe landing under these conditions ... well, that'll go over well during the annual performance review, I tell you what."

"No, I mean ... am I selling my soul here?"

Turbulence

The creature sighed again. "Always with the existentialism. Look, Jimmy-jam, did you ever think that it may not be all about angels, demons, souls and damnation? You get your ticket punched here, your run's over. That means a million little things don't happen, like your little girl's first dance with her daddy or giving your son his first driving lesson. And maybe one day that boy's not paying as close attention to where he's going, because he didn't have you to be a good teacher, and next thing you know he runs over some bum. Now he's in jail, the bum's dead, and a million more things that the boys way above my pay grade care about ain't gonna happen."

"That still doesn't explain why..."

"Why what? Why you get a little Charity? Like I said: there's a million little things I'm paid not to care about, and someone else is paid a lot more to make sure come true. This is one of those things. Hell, two of those things if you're keeping score. You've got me over a real barrel here, which is why the terms are so generous. Sometimes there's agreements for firstborns, maybe a rider to accept some kinda family curse, but not this one. This contract's a 100 percent, bona fide, *the wife's never gonna know about it* 'Get Out of A Horrible Death Free And Get Laid At the Same Time' card.'"

The thing leaned in, putting the pen into James' hand. "These deals don't come around that often. You're a lucky guy. Now do the smart thing, sign the paper, and go have a good time."

James looked at the pen. It felt far heavier than it should, and the onyx tip looked like it could cut through glass. He felt his seat vibrate as the plane hit a pocket of turbulence, and the creature looked out the window nervously.

"Almost there, Jimmy boy," it said. "Time to sign."

He licked his lips. "I ... I just don't know..."

The thing threw its claws up. "Come on, kid, you're making me nervous over here! You worried about protection, is that it?" It waved its hand, and a compartment over James' head snapped open: instead of a yellow nozzle and bag, a square of pink plastic fell into his hands.

"Ribbed for her pleasure," the thing leered. The plane continued to shudder around them. "Stick it in your wallet, and you're good to go."

James reached for his wallet in a haze. As he opened it, he saw a photo tucked behind his driver's license; he pulled the tiny image out, running his thumb over his wife's beaming face as she held two swaddled, crying bundles.

"She'll never know?" he asked.

Turbulence

The creature shook its head. "She'll be so happy you survived the crash she won't ever think twice. The thought will never once enter her happy, happy little mind."

James held the photo up to the light. Jessica's blonde, sweaty hair was stuck to the sides of her face as she grinned at the camera. The twins were both bawling, Valerie's pink face all scrunched up while Timothy's mouth formed a perfect 'O' of displeasure. He hadn't seen his wife ever smile like that in the ten years since their birth; she was always rushing to get them to school, or to a recital, or to a team practice or one of the other thousands of events they were involved in. Since James agreed to take on more consulting trips to help pad their budget they barely saw each other, and whenever they did they were both too exhausted to do much more than acknowledge each other and prepare for the next round of crises.

He looked at the picture of his family, then down at all the other pictures of the women who came before them; his entire checkered past spread out in front of him, each girl's eyes looking into his, either accusing, or blaming, or just wanting to know why. Why he never called, why he cheated on them, why he didn't live up to the image he left behind in their minds when he first met them.

James sighed, then put the picture back into his wallet.

The creature tapped its talons. "Clock's ticking, Jimmy," it said, "so man up and sign on the..."

"I'm not signing anything," he said defiantly.

The creature huffed. "I understand cold feet," it said hurriedly, "but you have just a few minutes before a ton of steel decides to turn you into chowder. You don't sign now, and I can't..."

"I reject your offer," James said, turning in his seat to face the creature. "I will not do what you ask."

It hissed like a snake, pushing the briefcase at him as the turbulence started bouncing their seats. "You're out of time, James," it said, "so stop trying to be the hero you aren't and take another one for the team!"

"I reject your offer," James shouted over the shaking aircraft, staring directly into the creature's coal-black eyes. "I reject your terms, I reject your reality, and your lies, and your truths, but most importantly *I reject you.*"

There was a flash of light from outside the window, and a gout of flame tore along the surface of the wing. Metal flared and shrieked as it was ripped apart, and the creature in front of James howled as the wall behind it suddenly buckled and sucked it out into the blue air. James felt the wind tearing at his skin as people screamed around him and felt the same plunging feeling in his gut as the row of chairs he was in suddenly heaved and was sucked out into open space...

* * * *

"Sir, we've landed. You can let go of the chair now."

James groggily opened his eyes. A stewardess with strawberry blonde hair ... *Charity*, her nametag said ... was shaking his shoulder.

"Are ... are we on the ground?" he asked weakly.

She smiled, a dazzlingly-white confirmation. "I know it got a bit bumpy back there, but you're all fine now. Need help with your carry-on?"

"No, I've got it," James said as he unbuckled his belt and stood up. His legs wobbled but stayed under him, and he looked back over his shoulder to the empty seat next to the window.

"Was there someone sitting here?" he asked.

The stewardess frowned. "No, you had the only seat in the row," she said. "We were a bit light this leg of the trip."

James nodded, rubbing his hand over his face. "I'm sorry," he said, "it's just been a long flight. Thank you."

"You're quite welcome," she said as she stepped aside to let him pass. The door to the cockpit opened as James approached the exit, and Charity watched the pilot stop and chat with him for a second before shaking his hand and wishing him well. She looked over at the two seats, and noticed a half-empty glass of ginger ale by the window. She reached over and took it, swirling it around thoughtfully before downing it in one swig.

The pilot walked toward her, taking off his hat and rubbing the sweat which had collected on his bald, shining forehead. "He rejected us. Again," he said, narrowing his solid-black eyes.

She frowned. "Give him time. He's only human, after all. We keep taking his memory, but the damage remains. His resolve will break sooner or later."

"We're running out of 'sooners'," the bald one pointed out. "The boys upstairs are starting to get unhappy."

"They'll get what they're after," she said, smiling slyly. "Don't forget, he still has to fly back home."

The Brazil Business

By Kevin Wright

Part 1: The Iron Embrace

Postmarked from:

Rio de Janeiro

Brazil

9 May 1930

My Dearest Brother Gilbert,

Please, allow me to assure you that I am not mad. Had I remained in Ipswich, that would have been madness.

In your last correspondence, you invoked Kate's name in some crude attempt to shame me to return, but you must understand two things: one, I do this for Kate, and two, I do this at the behest of Kate. I will not say that there is not some modicum of shame in all this for me, but such is the matter in these things. You should know it was she; it was Kate, who asked me — no, begged me, to go. It was her last wish, her only wish, her last words spoken on this earth. If only I could erase my last memory of her, that beautiful face, sunken, sallow, those green eyes once so full of verve, of life, laughter and splendor, now relegated to a dead gray, broken, lifeless. What cyclopean vistas those eyes will gaze upon to her last I shudder to ponder. And the rest of her, swallowed by that vile contraption. The doctors stood there, clipboards in hand, praising it as some miracle. I witnessed no miracle, only pain and shame and horror. Agony, there is no other word for it. Lord forgive me, brother. I am being horrible, I know it, saying such things, but Kate feels the same — felt the same. I could read it on her face even when she had not the strength or faculties to speak. It sat festering there in her eyes, a plea for release. Would that I were a man made of sterner stuff.

I suppose to understand my decision you would have to have children of your own. I mean this not as a slight, dear brother, but perhaps your recent difficulties can be viewed somehow as a blessing in this regard? But wait — it has been nearly a year and you have had my brood under wing for the lion's share of it. Perhaps in this time you have come to understand something of which I speak, something of which I have done? Yes, I think it so. I know it. It is a double-edged sword, though, is it not, brother? For to understand the path I tread is to tread it yourself. And I do not wish that upon you. I do not wish that upon anyone. Edward would not understand. He is not even married, the old bachelor. But you, brother, don't make my same mistakes. I beg this of you.

You said in your letter there is no winning this war. This was no secret kept from me, nor from Kate. Time was ever our greatest challenge, our greatest nemesis, insurmountable perhaps, but to not try was to not only court defeat, but wholly embrace it. That I could not do.

I pondered for more hours than I care enumerate on whether Kate knew it, so long ago. Indeed, yes, she suspected it; it has become clear to me now; were that it was clear to me then. I can see her now as we wandered, hand in hand, along the white dunes of Ipswich, the surf pounding below. I recall now a moment of weakness she had, a stumble, me catching her, and a sudden translucent paleness to her lovely skin that long days in the sun had done nothing to abate. It was her new parasol, she had explained, and I had believed. That lovely white parasol. Perhaps, I simply wanted to believe. Perhaps I am a fool. Perhaps what I am doing is foolish, but it is my only hope and Kate's last. She was always so much stronger than I, so much the wiser. On some level I wish I had regarded her beliefs with something more than … I simply wish I had listened to my wife. Her warnings fell upon deaf ears. How is it I can hear them now, tolling endlessly in my mind with the grim foreboding of funerary bells? The truth nearly breaks me. She did not wish to disappoint her foolish, loving husband. If Kate had one weakness besides the curse incubating within, it was her love for me. Gil, forgive me. That you must sit in for Father Paul, hearing this confession, reading my broken heart bled out in script upon this page. Do not fear, brother; my confession brings me no cure for my shame. That, I shall carry until the very end of my days.

If you should happen to have it within you to see Kate, kiss her on the cheek for me, and whisper in her ear that Wilbur loves her, and he labors for her, though he may be far away.

Your crusading brother,

Wilbur

P.S. You must send the sum I requested in my last letter, ASAP. Without it, all my labors are wasted.

Kevin Wright

Postmarked from:

    Ipswich, Massachusetts

    United States of America

    15 August 1930

To my brother Wilbur:

Your children are doing just fine. Fine as one might expect given their circumstances. I suppose amongst all your intrigues and adventures you must have forgotten to inquire of them.

Young Samuel turned ten, two weeks past. He remains a stodgy little man in the same vein as his old Uncle Edward. He inquired as to where you were and if you would be coming back soon. Perhaps for his birthday? I told him I didn't know. I wanted to tell him that I didn't know that you would ever be back, for that is what I truly believe. This damned Brazil business shall be the death of you. I know it. But I could not bring myself to. The lad has been through too much. He has grown so much in so short a time. But always so serious, so somber. Forgive me, Wilbur. We have always been so close. I do not say these things to hurt you, or I do, but I don't mean them. Not fully. We both partook in the DeLoy's expedition. Three years away in the heart of the boy's life, a blink of the eye to us. But to him? And now one more added to the tally. How many atop that in the end, brother? I think sometimes he sees himself as the father of this little band of yours. If this is true, he passes muster and then some. He watches out for Willa like a hawk. All three of them do. Clemens is a little ruffian, but a jovial one. And Henry, bookish Henry, who is most like your Kate; even he will rise from his precious studies to defend little Willa's honor. At Samuel's party, little Willa smeared a fistful of cake on one of the Lazarus boy's good jackets, the big one, Jeremy, I think. He chased Willa, her giggling the whole while, mind you, the little imp. All the way across the lawn and down to the river they ran. And like some scene from Camelot, the three little knights, your three little knights, tore after, tiny fists balled, howling for the Lazarus boy's blood. I was never so proud. I just wish that Samuel would hazard a smile, just once.

Yesterday, I visited with Kate at the Danvers Asylum, at your request, and did what you bade me. She looks the same. The same but paler, I suppose. She's always been so pale. The doctor says she has lost weight, which is hard to believe. Emily accompanied me, or I should restate, I accompanied her. It will hearten you to know that she goes there every day, rain or shine, so there is a friendly face and voice to attend Kate. Emily saw to it that her room was moved to the east wing. She now lies staring out a window, sunshine and a sea breeze, when the wind is right, upon her cheek. Emily brushes her hair and applies makeup for her, and generally does whatever else a nurse need do. The nurses allow her. It's a good thing, a good thing for Kate, I know. A good thing for Emily, I hope. It wears on her, I know, but she will brook no discussion of the matter. You would imagine a gap of eleven years would instill some sort of chasm between two siblings, but Kate and Emily? Always inseparable. Always. Small wonder they married twins, eh? Well…

I sent the five thousand dollars you requested. I can only imagine what it's for. I've a dark suspicion it involves Willoughby. I pray I am wrong, but then, you and I have always had that bond, that connection, and so I know it for truth. Please, promise me you will use it wisely. Tell me you will use it to return, but no, I know you will not. It is strange being apart from you for so long a time, brother. Not even during our college years was there this separation, though the distance between Boston and Arkham is not comparable to that of Brazil and New England. This damned business of yours. What's it all about? I just feel so damned useless here. I wish you would come back soon. The doctor says Kate hasn't much time, but then, you must know this.

The Brazil Business

I must go now. That little imp is begging me to play hide and seek with her, and I dare not suffer her wrath by delaying any further.

Farewell,

Gilbert

Kevin Wright

Postmarked from:

Rio de Janeiro

Brazil

18 October 1930

To my dear brother Gilbert,

I thank you for the sum. It was not only useful; it proved vital. The A.G.S. offered little more than a pittance at the start and had drawn out completely by the end. My other backers have evaporated. I apologize that I could not relay my plans to you in a previous letter. The security of the post in this country is suspect at best, the wire even worse. A trusted associate from the consulate shall post this a week after I've left. Tomorrow, I begin my trek.

My dear brother, I know your opinion of Dr Willoughby. You have made no bones of telling me since the days I labored as his research assistant, but I think you must reprise your thoughts on him, for you are in his debt in at least one regard. It was he that convinced me to put pen to paper and send this letter off to you, albeit, his reasoning was, as always, more pragmatic than sentimental. You'll find a sealed copy of my will enclosed. Dr Willoughby has explained the dangers of our trek, not that I am ignorant of them. But wait. You're still in the dark about all this. I told you before that everything I am doing is for my beloved Kate. I stand by this. Soon, I know you will, too.

Allow me to recommence. Allow me to explain. As you well know, my recent studies have solely concerned the forlorn and forgotten tribes of men of the upper Amazonia, with a concentration in their customs, their belief systems, religious, in particular. I think it no exaggeration to say that I am now one of the foremost scholars in this discipline. There are others, to be sure, but I believe I finally breathe the rarefied air.

And as you know, Dr Willoughby is the preeminent scholar in this same discipline. I know you will say that your Dr Scarsdale is of a commensurate stratification, but in my opinion, Scarsdale is lacking in the vital arena of field experience. How can one purport to be an expert on a people when one has never broken bread with them, never hunted by their side, never slept under the same roof? One cannot learn solely through books or artifacts, dear brother.

Proudly, I can say it was I that provided the spark that set our fevered journey ablaze. The long and short of it is this: I have made a discovery, an important discovery. It began within the realm your Dr Scarsdale holds most sacred, the pages of books. I was perusing Frazer's *Golden Bough* when a small passage concerning the rites of a tribe of Amazonians struck me. It caused a serendipitous itch within my mind. I can explain it no other way. Strange, for I had read that tiny tome numerous times before and cannot say I ever remembered reading that particular passage. But I must have. I believe my mind was more attuned to the subject matter due to my particular circumstances. Dr Willoughby concurred. After reading it, I recalled a similar passage from Von Juntz's *Unausprechlichen Kulten.* My thesis centered on that work, you will remember. Between the two I found many striking similarities. Separated by decades, they describe the same rites, if not the same exact tribe. Willoughby provided the third side of our triangle of study. For years he had heard whispers of an account of a conquistador who sailed up the Amazon circa 1540. For months we labored, searching geographical associations, historical societies, and old record halls. We finally struck gold in the flooded basement of a venerable government building in Teresopolis. In the account, the conquistador, whose name remains unknown due to the document's advanced state of decay, describes numerous tribes in his journey up the Amazon in search of that famous lost city of gold, El Dorado. I was concerned only with one tribe which he visited. In splendidly precise, if horrible detail, he describes the exact rite found in the aforementioned texts.

The Brazil Business

He even names the tribe, though I shall not repeat it here, for this discovery, should we uncover it, will prove immense. Here is the crux of it: all three accounts relate the same ritual, a ritual said to result in the prolonging of human life. The conquistador set out to find El Dorado, but seemingly found the Fountain of Youth!

"But brother," I can hear you say as I sit here, sipping a dram of rum. "These are but tales. Jungle folklore. Stories passed down through the ages. Where is the proof?" Yes, my brother, you scholar, you desire proof, and proof you shall have. It was Dr Willoughby who provided it. As I said before, he is a scholar unafraid of grinding out time in the field. Well, he relates a curious story. Did I ever tell you that Dr Willoughby was a personal acquaintance of that doomed explorer Colonel Percy Fawcett, who disappeared some five years ago in the wilds of Amazonia, in search of his mythical City of Z? Well, he was. I've seen a picture of the two, standing shoulder to shoulder, both chewing pipes, both wearing those ridiculous hats bent at rakish angles. They met while Colonel Fawcett was describing the western border of Bolivia. Dr Willoughby was imbedded with a tribe in the northwest of that country, studying their hunting techniques. Dr Willoughby says he saved Fawcett's life when the steely-eyed Englishman, raging with fever, practically stumbled into the tribe's camp. Were it not for Dr Willoughby, Fawcett would surely have succumbed to the fever, or worse. The tribesmen were cannibals.

Brother ... Dr Willoughby has seen Colonel Fawcett, and only months ago. The man dozens of others have trekked to find, all having failed. He has seen the man who disappeared in the very section of Amazonia I mean to explore, the very section my tribe inhabits. And here it is, brother; Willoughby swears that Colonel Fawcett appeared as though he were twenty years younger than when last they met. I ask you, what is this if not proof? The Colonel has found his City of Z, or El Dorado in the common parlance. He has found the tribe; he has taken part in this rite. It has to be. It can only be. And I ask you, if such proof can be found, uncovered, harnessed, would it not be the panacea to all of humanity's ills? Would it not do the same for my beloved Kate? I pray it is so, for I depart tomorrow morning.

Your crusading brother,

Wilbur

The Brazil Business

Postmarked from:

    Ipswich, Massachusetts

    United States of America

    25 December 1930

My dear Brother Wilbur,

Forgive me. There is no other way to say this, Will; your beloved Kate is beyond all help. She succumbed to her malady early this very morning, passing beyond the veil. My steadfast Emily sat by her side through it all; that, I hope, is some comfort. It is to me, at least. We have not told the children, so as to preserve this Yuletide memory for them. We do not wish to taint it in their hearts for the sum total of their years with this quiet aura of death. I don't know if it is right, but it is what we have decided. She went quietly, Emily said, like into a long peaceful rest, eyes simply closing, never to reopen, the machine encasing her in iron yet breathing for her. Emily had the doctor turn it off and remove her from it. And listen, Emily swears that the merest trace of a smile crooked the corners of Kate's lips when she was finally free of that iron embrace. I care not to over analyze it; I merely hope it is true. She will be cremated four days hence, her ashes spread to the winds upon the high dunes overlooking the sea you two loved so dear. It is a beautiful spot, and I hope that you and she shared many a happy memory there. It is a place worthy of her if any place of this earth is.

I will give you a summation of the children though you failed to ask of them again in your last missive. It is all good news. I need to write good news.

Young Samuel is doing better though he does not believe in Santa Claus anymore. Fear not, it was not as bad as all that. I don't know how he found out, another child from school; one of those scoundrel Lazarus boys, I suspect. He questioned me about it one night, a month past, upon a dark night in lonesome November. He questioned me in the manner of a man, and I did not have it in me to continue the lie. He asked like a man; he took it like a man. I feared for him, his reaction, as I'm sure you are reading this. Would it break him? So to soften the blow, I took him on board, as they say, asking him to be part of my clandestine little operation. I made him swear an oath, and he did so, hand over heart, without reservation. Listen: he pretends to still believe as much for Emily's sake — I've yet to tell her — as for appearances before Clemens, Henry, and Willa. And he smiled last night on Christmas Eve! A more glorious present I have never received, nor could ever have hoped to even ask for. He and I are compatriots in this whole glorious deception. Picture this: it was like some spy pulp of the great game, and he and I were operatives slinking through some obscene Thuggee temple in an effort to abscond with a treasured pagan idol. Slinking headfirst down the stairs, peeking around corners, present-engorged satchels slung about our shoulders, we made our way through the darkness to that pagan eidolon, the Christmas tree. Without a sound we stacked the presents, creating structures worthy of the Mayans, gasping at every creak, every rattle of wind against shutter. You'll be glad to know we met with resounding success. Not a peep from the rest of the brood. Our mission completed, we returned to our respective rooms, silently saluting before retiring. But in the dark, after we laid down those presents, briefly, by candlelight, I saw that smile upon his face, that smile I have not seen in ages. It was brilliant! I almost whooped like a wild Indian. I would have told him the truth years before had I known how he'd take to it. Bless him. Bless them all.

The others are doing well, too. Clemens is still a ruffian, and will always be a ruffian, I suspect. Henry and Emily have their own little book club and read every night. They're reading a Jules Verne novel right now, his most beloved Christmas present, the story about the submarine that runs on the power of the atom. I think it's a bit much for him; I worry the dreams that have plagued me of late, of tentacled things writhing in the in the deep, will infect him, but Emily insists he loves it, and I have not the will to take away from any of them. And Willa, she has shot up in height seemingly overnight, surpassing young Henry by an inch if not more. She finds no end to the hilarity of it all. Henry, by contrast, is dour about the whole situation, but he gets on. Clemens has been threatening her to stop growing lest she outstrip him, too, but I know he does not mean it. Those two scoundrels are peas in a pod.

I pray you are safe, and that this letter reaches you, wherever you are. I worry about you every day. I wish I were by your side, trekking through the unknown, a machete in hand and backpack on shoulder, my trusty forty-five holstered at my hip.

Brother, I have relayed the majority of your previous letter to Dr Scarsdale. He restated many points that I had in mind as I read it. Please, take heed.

Firstly, Willoughby is a scoundrel. I care not to call him doctor. Dr Scarsdale says the man would sell his soul for even publication in any scientific journal. What would he sell to be part of a discovery? I believe Dr Scarsdale. He says that men in Willoughby's parties have a habit of going "missing" with an alarming frequency. Dr Scarsdale makes no claims to incidences of foul play, but he cannot rule them out, and states bluntly that he would not be shocked in the least if such claims were proven true.

Secondly, Colonel Fawcett disappeared five years ago. He is dead. The man that Willoughby claims to have seen is most likely just that, a claim, or in more common parlance, a bold-faced-lie. Dr Scarsdale states he has heard this very same story through the grapevine of academia — yes, Miskatonic and Harvard dwell within that same hermetic microcosm, despite your opinion of the latter — and it has been laughed at, at best. At worst? I will say only that Willoughby is a sinking ship, and I pray you are not aboard, or even nearby when finally he sinks, for fear that you will be sucked down into the deep along with him.

Thirdly, even were Willoughby's claim not a lie, and he did indeed see "Colonel Fawcett," could it not have been his son, Jack, or even his compatriot, Raleigh, both whom accompanied him? To my recollection, father and son bore similar aspects, and their age difference was roughly twenty-five years. Twenty and twenty five years is but a trifling gap. I know you must have considered this. Know, too, that I have only the highest opinion of you, but I think in matters concerning Willoughby you have a blind spot. I pray only you keep him in sight, and never at your back.

Lastly, this fountain of youth business... Do you truly believe in this day and age of science and innovation that the extension of life might be garnered through the study of savage rite and ritual? If such miracles are to be found, surely it will be under the eye of a microscope, within the cell matter of a nuclei and the chromosomes beyond. What you search for does not exist, brother. I can understand your pain and sorrow, but I cannot

understand your reasoning. I wish only that you realize this and that you return safely, if not swiftly.

Farewell,

Gilbert

P.S. More good news: Emily shared a second birthday present with me, the day after Christmas. Your four hoodlums are soon to have a cousin.

The Brazil Business

Part 2: Dead Horse Camp

Postmarked from:

Cuiaba

Brazil

16 February 1931

To my dear brother Gilbert,

I received your letter early this morning. My thanks. It does ease my heart to know that your Emily was with my dear Kate when she passed. It eases it to no end, my sole source of solace in this accursed, sweatbox jungle. I can only imagine what this whole affair has wrought upon the two of you. The strain it must have caused. By God, I wish that I could have been there, could be there now. Even to see her that one last time, passed beyond, but slipped free of that prison for even that briefest of moments. Your Emily saw her smile in the end, and that bolsters me. I can see that smile whenever I close my eyes. Thank Emily for me, will you, dear brother? No amount of gratitude I could offer would be commensurate to the deeds she has done, but thank her for me, nonetheless. You are both so strong, and it emboldens me that the strength that resides within you might lurk in some deep recess within me as well. I have need of such strength.

The trek here was arduous and not without its commensurate miseries and mishaps. Mishaps. Now I am using the word. An innocuous word, no? Brother, there may be some truth to what you wrote of Willoughby. Some truth, indeed. My eyes are open now, have no fear. Strange, too, it is that in your last letter you mentioned the sinking of a ship, for the ferry bearing us upriver met with just such a disaster. And your dreams, those dark dreams plaguing you of late, proved prescient as well.

Our ferry embarked, treacherously overladen with passengers, for Cuiaba, 160 miles south, our expeditionary crew along with it. Bodies were packed in so tightly I imagine the lower decks were somewhat akin to the slave ships plying the Caribbean in the 1800's. It happened in the dead of night, something striking the ship's hull a blow so severe it must have quaked the very earth. Hurled awake from my bunk, I smashed across the heaving floor, the shattering blow still reverberating aftershocks through the hull while the engine block cracked and pistons seized, all this cacophony painted upon the bleak canvas of the pitiful screams and pounding of those trapped below. Then we capsized.

The Brazil Business

In the sweltering dark I slammed into the wall and then ceiling all amidst the groaning squeal of failing metal, the salt-stink of sweat and tumbling bodies. Then came the water. An abyssal mountain of inevitability, it swept me tumbling from the dying vessel and into the wretched blackness beyond. It was almost a relief, almost; there is no blackness more complete than that of the Amazonian night. Helpless within the breathless suffocating swirl, I knew I must die. Kate's face before me I saw, and those of the children, as my heart and head threatened implosion through hypoxia, and then, when I could bear no more, I broke the water's surface.

We of the expedition, our berths lying on the topmost deck, were lucky, or I should reiterate, some of us were lucky. Some were not. Taken. There is no other word for it. There is no firm number, only estimate, conjecture, but Willoughby surmises as many as two hundred were lost in the 'mishap.' His word. The locals say it was something else; they speak in hushed tones of dead gods and river demons.

Nonsense, I can hear you say it.

But listen! As I treaded water on that blackest of nights, the ferry teetering on the edge of the abyss, with only the Southern Cross above, man, woman, and child flailing all about me, I felt it. Oh, Gil, the screams, their terrible gurgling wails, and the splashing. The river was calm there, serene almost. But something was in the water. Something I cannot describe. As the something slid past my body, undulating, I froze, and I prayed. Yes, by reflex and by rote, I prayed. The Lord's Prayer I recited, eyes squeezed shut, body frozen but trembling as this something continued sliding, slipping, oozing past. It ceased sliding across me the instant I finished the prayer. I have timed myself praying, many times since that night. Insane, yes. But twelve seconds. Ten if I were praying as swiftly as I could. Ten seconds. How fast careened that thing through the abyss? How big? I shudder to estimate. I can say only that by the grace of God am I still alive.

Brother, I thought myself in hell as I treaded water, disoriented, sputtering, half-drowned, listening to them all scream. I thought there would never be anything worse than that, the screaming, but the silence that followed was. One by one, a splash and a squeal and then one less ... one less ... one less. I soon swam on alone and in silence, wondering when I would be dragged down drowning into the deep. I swam as fast as I could, as long as I could, on through the darkness, the blessed Southern Cross above me the only fixed point for navigation, orientation, and it lead me to salvation, or so I had thought. Perhaps it led to but another layer of Dante's Hell?

Eighteen of the forty from the expedition survived that night. Downtrodden, but nevertheless alive, we gathered in the pale light of early morn along with some twenty other survivors. I literally had to pry the ferry's lifeboat from Willoughby's hands to start a search effort, a rescue effort, a recovery effort. Threefold, there was nothing to search for, nothing to rescue, nothing to recover. Nothing ... nothing ... and nothing. The fishermen who dragged the river found no shoal to founder on, no craft to collide with. Hundreds of feet of line they played out hand over hand over the side, sounding the depths. Dredging. Miles downriver. They found nothing.

Willoughby excoriated the fishermen for incompetent, superstitious fools. Willoughby, who prowled the riverbank throughout, helping not, admonishing the time wasted. At his side, ever-present, hanging thick as thieves, slink his two native guides. To look upon them one would think them identical twins, as you and I, only younger by a decade, but Willoughby just smirks and shakes his head when I ask. They linger in the shadows, their eyes goggle-wide, unblinking and staring, accusatory, their pronounced under-bites and strange filed teeth reminiscent of some forlorn sea lamprey. They speak a pidgin-slurry of Portuguese, English, and some native tongue that seems constructed predominantly of sibilant slurps and harsh, clicking fricatives. Willoughby insists they are stolid folk and necessary to complete the trek, for they hail from this forlorn tribe we seek; so we must suffer them. Willoughby's choice of the word 'suffer' seems apt.

Willoughby. I don't like this man since we left the city, this new man. There is a grim darkness to him I never witnessed before, an intensity burning, a haughty disregard for anything in his way. A Jekyll and Hyde transformation, to be sure. Were I to start this venture over, I would do so alone. But I must press on. In for a penny, in for a pound, 'they' say. What stakes then would 'they' say I am in for if in the penny's stead I had placed my very soul? For that is what I somehow sense I am doing, brother.

Farewell,

Wilbur

P.S. Inside, you will find a codicil amended to my last will and testament.

The Brazil Business

Postmarked from:

    Ipswich, Massachusetts

    United States of America

    12 April 1931

My brother Wilbur,

Are you mad? I posited this same question to you three missives ago and you assured me you were not. I placated you at the time, for you believed, however erroneously, that you were trekking to save your dear Kate's life, however long the odds, however ridiculous your reasoning, however it broke and battered your children's psyches. I can stand by no more and see this thing done. The children need a father. They need an intact father, and I fear that if you continue on this venture, even if somehow you should return, you will prove yourself more a burden to them than bulwark. I fear you should become something unrecognizable to them, though they gaze upon your visage through me every day.

And again! Again you have failed to ask of them. What are they to you? Are they nothing? They are your flesh and your blood. They are all that will remain of you when you are dust. They are all that remains of Kate. Not even to mention the news I post-scripted in my last offering. But no, you are too consumed for such matters. Well, I shall tell you anyways. Emily is doing just fine. She is nearly five months on and just starting to show, a miraculous healthy glow about her.

Your children, however, are a different matter entirely. Samuel and Clemens are doing well; there is that. It is Henry who has suffered the blow. A spiral fracture to his left femur, according to Doctor Harris, a very bad break. He is in bed, in traction constantly. The doctor questioned me upon mechanism of the injury and strenuously refused to believe what I told him. He and Willa were horsing around when I heard the snap. I couldn't believe it at first. Henry just had a confused look on his face for a moment; then he began clutching, clutching and screaming. And as badly as I felt for him at the time, it is now for Willa that I feel worse. Henry cried and wailed, but Willa. Poor Willa. She just stared at her hands and uttered not a sound. For three days she spoke not at all. She just sat up there in her room, silent and by turns crying, whimpering. To see a girl of her high spirits laid so low desiccated my very soul. It was all I and Emily could do to get her to finally venture forth from her domain. But she is like a changed person and refuses to visit Henry.

Henry, the good lad, bears no malice for the event; the boy carries a stiff upper lip. Strange it is that he is by turns both the weakest of the group and the strongest. In retrospect, I suppose it best that it was he that suffered this calamity; the other three would go mad laid up as he is. He, at least, can retreat into the realms of his beloved books. Emily has retreated along with him; the two of them lie there in bed most of the day, amidst a dizzying array of steel rods and ropes and pulleys, reading to each other their favorite tales. I hear them laughing as I write this. It is a beautiful music to my ear, to hear these two bonding, healing, but there is also something disconcerting. Perhaps because Henry I've always seen as being closest to Kate in both visage and temperament. It concerns me of other matters, a fell wind, so to speak, that I care not to dwell long upon.

I have returned to work at the Peabody Museum of Salem and took work teaching at your alma mater, Miskatonic University. I know you will have some crowing about the lowering of their standards, hiring a Harvard man for anything above janitorial services, and all. It was but a simple equation: they needed a crypto-anthropology professor, and I needed money. Scandalous, I know, but finances have been abysmal since the downfall of the market. The work has refocused me, and the added money is a much needed blessing though I fiercely miss the time spent with the children.

Edward took a drubbing, worse than us, in the market crash. He lost the stocks, the business, the home; he lost everything, even that sacred gun collection of his in the end was whittled away to nothing but an old rusted flintlock piece from the Revolutionary War. Emily grumbles about him, the brother who had the temerity to miss our wedding over a business matter. We have taken him in though we tell the children he has only come to visit us, a vacation of sorts. An effort to maintain his dignity, you see. But Samuel knows. Sharp lad that he is, he asked, and I told. The others don't suspect a thing; they are simply glad to finally meet their erstwhile uncle. They adore him in his gruff, curmudgeonly ways and, more surprisingly, he they. It seems to have done wonders for him. The old beast even smiles on occasion, imagine that. He's teaching them fly fishing and boxing, his two loves. Not Henry, of course, but Edward sits upon the edge of Henry's bed telling him of the time he sat ringside while Victor McLaglen and Jack Johnson boxed for six rounds in a whiskey barn up in Canada. Emily disapproves of such fare, but it may be because she has been dethroned; Henry has a new hero.

Anyways … forgive me for this letter's beginning. My flaming ire has burned clean, leaving only the noisome fumes of anxiety and remorse. I did not sleep a wink the night I read your last letter; it haunted me for days. It haunts me still. But your eyes are open now, and that is something. That is something, indeed. I shall end this letter as I always shall. Come back, brother, come back to your family. Your children need their father.

Your brother,

Gilbert

Kevin Wright

Postmarked from:

Dead Horse Camp

via Cuiaba

Brazil

14 May 1931

My Dearest Brother Gilbert,

Can you not see? My children have a father, and though he is not the biological one, he is the one, by far, more suited to the task. You did not ask for this burden; I know. For that I am truly sorry. You accused me before of blindness with regards to Willoughby and correctly so. It is now that I must turn the tables on you, dear brother, though it pains me to do so. For you are blind, as well, with regard to two subjects: my four children and your soon to be son or daughter.

Do you remember our high school biology class with old Professor Ziminski? When first we were introduced to that precursor to the modern day study of genetics? Of course, I speak of Gregor Mendel's eugenics and his Laws of Inheritance. Oh, how we lamented those damned peas, and charts, and X's and Y's. An apt lesson it was, though, in retrospect. Listen: Kate had warned me, before we were wed, of her family curse, of the degenerative disorder that has riddled and stunted the Marsh family tree through the generations, taking out whole branches, that degenerative, sickening, killing disease. But Kate, dear Kate, she cared not a whit about herself; she cared only for the health of the children, and watched over them with a loving eye, a loving eye full of dread and of mounting trepidation.

I assumed that Emily had warned you as well. Clearly, she had not. And now it is too late. You and she have rolled the dice, as had we. They tumble still. Of course, I pray for a good outcome. I pray for you; I pray for Emily; I pray for the baby. I pray to the gods of recessive genes and beg that they remain recessed. My four have given me more joy and happiness than I ever thought possible, but my worry for them is consuming, bottomless, inexhaustible. And now yours is as well.

You admonished me for not writing of them, of not inquiring of them. Can you not see that it wrenches my very soul to give them thought? Can you not see they are the very Sword of Damocles hanging over my head? Should I give pause, lose momentum, stumble, it will be my last. For that is the only certainty here. Death. Death in every shade and every form, in every flora and fauna, in every river and jungle. And what minutiae the jungle may lack in this deadly regard, man most assuredly bears along with him. I am staring at that very minutiae as I write.

Guns. Willoughby still possesses his guns, all of the guns in the party; he sits by the fire with his two squids (as I refer to the twin guides now, it is apt, trust me), each cleaning a rifle, their wide eyes glistening, staring, always staring. How are those guns not lying at the bottom of the river along with the rest of the party's equipment? How Willoughby accomplished this feat fosters more questions in my mind than answers. In the black of night, amidst the rolling hulk, how is it possible for a man to save all of those supplies? Guns. Food. How to get them on the lifeboat? How even to get the lifeboat? I would call it Herculean, but I think that inappropriate. I call it impossible.

Across our divided camp I can hear Willoughby's conversation as I scribble this note. I can decipher some of their gibberish now. And what I can garner offers me no solace. Listen, one of the two squids refers to the other by the moniker 'father.' Can the two truly be father and son? Is this mounting evidence of eternal life? The Fountain of Youth? It may seem strange, but these two seemingly youthful squids fill me with a kind of dreadful hope. And I have deciphered another piece of the puzzle from their conversations. They talk at length of the Pale King. What it means I know not. Is it in reference to Colonel Fawcett? The

The Brazil Business

Anglican king of their native jungle tribe? His son Jack? Or Jack's boon companion, Raleigh Rimmell? Or is it someone, or something else?

We have been in the jungle on foot for over a week now. We achieved Dead Horse Camp early this morn, the last known location of Colonel Fawcett before his trek into the deep jungle. Eighteen men we started out with from Cuiaba; now seven sit here in camp. They are disappearing like the petals of a dying rose; they wilt and wither and then fall away, one by one, never to be seen again. Desertion, no doubt, has taken its toll, as have other oddities of misfortune.

One of the porters was taken in the Upper Xingu by what the natives call a 'lau lau,' a great whiskered leviathan. The man was bathing when it took him, crushing his torso in its massive jaws before swallowing him whole. Twelve feet long and in the split of a blink it was there and then gone, the porter with it. I did not know his name. He had a hearty laugh and a strong back. I shall miss his laugh. I think he had a wife and child; I am not certain. And this was nothing. Steel yourself, brother.

Another man, Joshua Weeks, a dour Australian chap, was taken by the bugs. Four days ago he slipped and fell up to his neck in a mire. The natives called it a mosquito pit. Weeks lamented on about it as we, laughing, drew him free. Yesterday he did not laugh. Nor we. Yesterday, patches all about his body began to swell in the hundreds. It became clear the swelling was not some allergic reaction, as we had first surmised. You see, the tumors began to move, inching along through him, creeping beneath his flesh. I have never witnessed fear in man's eyes as I did in his. Not even in the trenches of France when the phosgene and chlorine mists rolled over, engulfing us in poisoned silence. Not even then. Riddled with the things, infested, Weeks devolved into nothing more than a seething mass of the pale wriggling things, their shiny black beaks piercing free, each one akin to some hellish baby bird, chirping and begging from its hideous nest, amidst his thrashes and groans. We tore at them, burned the cursed things with brands, smashed them under foot and stone. We considered what to do, and could only come to one inevitable course of action. We drew straws for it, the time-honored tradition in the face of truly bleak decisions. I drew shortest. That bastard Willoughby would not consent to '*wasting*' precious ammunition on a '*procedure*' that might be accomplished through less expensive means. Nonetheless it was over quickly. Weeks had a Christian burial. I will say no more.

The Brazil Business

Barring future catastrophe, this shall be the last letter I write for some time and yours the last I receive. The jungle runners, carrying supplies as well as posts, dare travel no further than here. They had to be paid an exorbitant sum to come even this far, and we had lost near everything in the wreck, but to travel light is to travel fast, and to travel far.

Farewell,

Wilbur

Kevin Wright

Postmarked from:

Ipswich

Massachusetts

United States of America

12 August 1931

My Dear Brother Wilbur,

It has been six months since your last missive. I am writing this, sealing it, and posting it with every expectation for it never to reach your hands, never to be opened, your eyes never to set upon it. I write it nonetheless. I have to do something. Writing letters seems a poor substitute for action, but there it is; it is all I can do.

I contacted a Mr. Daniel Ellsworth at the U.S. consulate in San Paulo in regards to the situation. I explained that you have gone missing. I explained the circumstances of your trek, the last city you posted from, Cuiaba, and your last known location, this Dead Horse Camp of Colonel Fawcett's renown. Mr. Ellsworth responded very cordially, was very encouraging, and very useless. He explained to me that he was not wholly ignorant of your travels, and that it was he that you and Willoughby dealt with in regards to obtaining the various permits and bribes necessary for 'your little trek into the woods,' as he put it. I have sent this letter to Mr.

The Brazil Business

Ellsworth; he gives me his best assurances that he will see that it reaches your hand the moment you set foot out of the jungle. His assurances are not reassuring.

Edward has gone after you. One of us had to do something. Over a bottle of brandy we argued over courses of action. My course was to board the soonest trawler and set sail for Brazil on the next tide. Edward agreed, wholeheartedly, his one caveat being that it be him and not I that set sail. Stalemated, we came nearly to blows over it when, out of nowhere, he pulled the trump card of the ages. A nasty business, he told Emily. Over the previous months the two had fought like cats and dogs over even the most inconsequential of items. On this they were of one mind. The decision was made in the blink of an eye. Edward would crusade on alone.

He embarked at the end of July by the cattle ship *Cartagena* (Edward insisted on remaining until the birth of our son, Wilbur, a rude, noisy chap named after his rude, noisy uncle, and stood in your stead at the Christening), that old battered suitcase of his in hand, the wanderer's gleam twinkling in his eye. I gave him my old .45, for if I cannot be there in person, perhaps a part of me travels to you. Doctor Scarsdale, expert that he is in Amazonian cultures and linguistics, agreed to accompany him when we apprised him of the situation. It lightens my heart to know Edward will not be alone. The children were sorry to see him go, as was Emily (their alliance against me has fused the two feuding parties into a strangely harmonious one), as was I. I yearned to be aboard that old cantankerous ship alongside those old cantankerous men, amidst the braying stink and squalor, to come to your rescue, to see you again and perhaps to aid you in your quest.

I worry. In my dreams, you huddle stooped in the dark, surrounded by the cloying stench of rotting fish, degenerate shadows cavorting before firelight upon some slick subterranean wall. And I hear water dripping, always. I think you are not dead, brother. I think I would know. Perhaps it would be a strange thing to say to another, but I know you would understand.

Part of me wishes this letter never finds you. I would spare you the pain if it were in my power. Henry's condition has not improved. There it is. It has been months and the leg has not healed as it should. It was a severe break, yes, but no progress has been made. I fear for him. What you and I wrote of, somewhat cryptically in our last letters, and what the doctors know but will not tell me, what has re-broken my poor Emily's heart, I shall now write plainly. Henry carries the Marsh family curse. I have always known it, I think, just as have you. The doctors perform their interminable tests and hide behind clipboards their looks of consternation to one another, all the while patting me tepidly on the shoulder and telling me to keep my chin up. But that same pale translucence that brought Kate low is now upon the boy. I know this letter shall never reach you, but you must know, you must overcome what obstacles detain you; you must hurry. You must accomplish this mission of yours. For Henry now you must succeed. You must. You must. You must.

Farewell,

Gilbert

Kevin Wright

Postmarked from:

    Mr. Daniel P. Ellsworth

    United States Consulate

    Rio de Janeiro

    Brazil

    18 August 1931

Dear Mr. Gilbert Webb Hawkins:

It is only with the sincerest regret that I must inform you of the death of your brother.

A Doctor Willoughby, Emeritus of Miskatonic University, a member of you brother's party…

Part 3: The Pale King

Postmarked from:

Ipswich

Massachusetts

United States of America

30 August 1931

My dear brother Edward,

A nightmare week past, I received a letter from the U.S. consulate notifying me of the death of our dear brother Wilbur. There it is. It grieves me to have to tell you this in a letter. It grieves me to have to punctuate, for you, the end of Wilbur's very existence with nothing more than a dot of ink, the merest mote at the end of a sentence. To have him snatched away into oblivion by something so mundane as boilerplate... He would laugh at it; I know he would, but I fear it has broken me. I cannot think. I cannot express. I cannot act. I cannot. I cannot. I cannot. That is who I am, now, someone who cannot.

You have set off toward your death in my place, at my bequest, and disappeared as well. Forgive me. I, the Luddite, have even resorted to sending you innumerable wires, and have received none in return. I have not slept, have not eaten and have nearly set up camp outside the wire station. For their part, the stations I have wired all swear by the God Almighty that they have gone through Herculean efforts to ascertain the location of your whereabouts. I can only trust they are sincere and not hyperbolic in their efforts.

The U.S. Consulate, too, remains ignorant of your whereabouts, though they state they are actively searching for you. Brother, they use the word, '*manhunt*,' and claim you are a wanted felon.

I know this for a mistake. A horrible mistake. I pray Dr Scarsdale remains by your side, wherever you may be. I have wired and written all of Brazil's major universities and reached the same conclusion in finding him as I have you. Jesus Christ! What the hell is going on? Where are you? And what were we thinking, sending that gentle soul into the heart of darkness? Lord, forgive me.

So I posted this letter as some insurance measure against my continued failure in locating you. I've posted copies to every hotel, hostel, and rooming house, every police station, and local official's office I could reach within a hundred miles of Cuiaba.

In my heart of hearts I feared from the start this crusade a fool's errand, at best. Feared? No. I knew. But it should have been me. Again. And at worst? '*At worst*' has now come to pass. The object of our crusade is no longer attainable. Come home, big brother, by whatever means necessary. Perhaps you can even return before poor, dear Henry...

Please, just come home.

Your stalwart brother,

Gilbert

Kevin Wright

Postmarked from:

Cuiaba Penitenciaria

Cuiaba

Brazil

16 December 1931

Dear Gilbert,

I have not slept in days, weeks. How many? I have lost track. Lost count. Closing my eyes brings ... I do not want to sleep, do not want to close my eyes. I fear the dark now, and it is always dark here.

I received your letter ... and I received your letter ... and I received your letter, forwarded to me from every hotel, every fleabag hostel, every embarkation, every shithole and festering piss-hole between Cuiaba and the sea. Consulate officials and local constables accosted me the moment I set foot from the jungle. Never have I been so thankful to be so accosted by so many bureaucrats. It was short-lived. As you have no doubt guessed, I write this from prison, and I tell you up front, I am guilty of the crime, that crime being murder. That is now, but you must steel yourself, little brother, and listen, for I've a grim story to tell...

Your Dr Scarsdale and I arrived in Rio de Janeiro on the first of August, and ferried on up the coast, then upriver to

The Brazil Business

Cuiaba to commence our search. Imagine us, two proper Yankee gents stumbling about some sweltering jungle metropolis in the dim hopes of gleaning any hint or clue of Wilbur's clandestine trek and subsequent disappearance, months gone past. An impossible task, I recall myself saying to Scarsdale during our overseas debates. Heady days, those, when existed things I still thought impossible.

Impossible? No, I give you a better word, *inevitable*. For not only did we garner a clue, but it was thrust neatly into our faces practically the moment we disembarked, plastered across the front page of some garish Cuiaba scandal sheet. It was Scarsdale who saw it. Like a hammer blow to the temple it halted him stunned-dead in his tracks. The headline read: *Cannibal Assassino!* Accompanying this grim line, which even I had the wherewithal to translate despite my deficiencies in the local tongue, was one of those lurid portraits sketched in the pencil scribblings of some crude police artist; the face leering from the page, heavy-lidded and ominous, of high breeding laid somehow low, somehow degenerate. Willoughby.

There was no discussion about it. Without pause, Scarsdale and I notified the local constabulary. Sly smirking uniformed men, junta men, they considered our words, our motives, with the natural suspicion and contempt any of the natives hold for light-skinned outsiders, intruders. No doubt Willoughby's present activities had done little to assuage them on that score.

Coin of the realm loosened tongues, however (Bribery seems a matter of course down here, being the sole comfort it shares with home).

There were some rather gruesome details to the affair — Jesus Christ — I am not even referring to the cannibalism, for in my mind, at this time, it seems somehow mundane, somehow ... quaint, for lack of a better world. How far gone am I...? According to the constables, in a hellish state of fevered lust, Willoughby had left a calling card in the form of runes etched into the flesh of his many victims, each one a woman of ill-repute. Each rune consisted of a series of stabbed dashes not unlike Morse code, but in place of straight lines, set in a series of ever widening concentric rings, all surrounding a central puncture mark. These were repeated, numerous times, dozens of times upon each victim. The constable believed they'd most likely been cut into the flesh with a razor blade and ice pick. None of them could ascertain its meaning, and did not truly care, for civil war was brewing, and Willoughby was no longer their problem. He had moved on upriver.

The Brazil Business

In a town — no — not a town, in a festering shit-hole called Sangue de Peixes we finally found him. And I'll not call it an orphanage, for it does the spirit of the institution no justice, but that was where we found him, nonetheless. Willoughby had changed his feeding — his modus operandi. Mother of God. Despite what he had become, still he was able to present an outwardly nonthreatening appearance. He was erudite, well-spoken, and very convincing, charming even. Well, he did some convincing, some charming at the orphanage, and he did more.

By the time we found him, he had been holed up in the basement nearly a week. Even now, at the time of this writing, months past, when I close my eyes I am once again in that concrete tomb, twin rows of support columns disappearing in the long quiet. Water dripping. The air thick, musty. A sudden scream then, a harpy's keen, drew us on through that endless labyrinth, a pair of electric torches our only means of navigation, of warding off the coffin dark. We hurdled onward, a strange buzz filling our ears.

We arrived just in time. Just in time…? I just wrote that. Nay. Not in time. We saved a child. One. How many did we *not* save? A week's worth of work. I could not count them. I did not try. The buzz was deafening here, ringing in my ears like the cacophony of a chainsaw ripping. And he was there.

Swarmed by a halo of buzzing black flies, slaughterhouse deep in rotting carcasses, Willoughby huddled. Degenerate. Deformed. Demented. Vulture-crouched over something struggling, something screaming, he fed. But our sudden intrusion startled him — his orphan prey tore kicking free and scrambled screaming into Scarsdale's outstretched arms.

Then he arose, Willoughby, shorn of all cloth and cloak, clad only in crimson horror. Finally, we deciphered the runes, understood them, for we beheld the tools used in their making. They had not been etched with steel as the constable surmised. They were bite marks. Cobra-like erect, long roping tendrils slithered furious about this nightmare incarnate, a whipping serpentine tangle of slick adders sprouting haphazard from Willoughby's chest and stomach and below. Upon the blunt end of each grinned a lamprey-like toothed-maw, a circular sucking gash wreathed by a ring of chitinous teeth.

The child screamed in Scarsdale's arms, and he stood there, frozen, the Lord's prayer murmuring upon his lips, a crucifix held shaking in his outstretched hand.

"Doctor Scarsdale…?" Willoughby lisped, squinting into the stunning torch-glare, a hand up, shielding his eyes as he oozed forth liquid from the black. Dead-soulless-white, like some blind cave-thing he stared, but I knew he could see, knew he did not like the light. Forward and aloft I thrust the torch, and he shied away like some damned thing, some monstrous child of Cain.

"Doctor Scarsdale..." Thumbing back the hammers on my double-barrel shotgun slung about my shoulder, I didn't turn ... I didn't move ... I simply said, "Run." And he did, turning, sprinting, the child clutched firmly within his arms.

Willoughby was upon me then. Snarling. Slathering. But the levelled twin-barrels mule kicked, emptying into him point blank, an explosion of scale and shorn tendril writhing. Once he spun, a devil's pirouette — but still — still on he came, this gnashing, twisted horror, tangling about me as I stepped forth into nightmare, swinging the empty shotgun like a Frankish war-axe, hacking into his face. Teeth exploded. Bone broke. But tentacle engulfed me, sliding across my flesh, pinning my arms, biting, squirming, squealing red. I cried out.

The bastard had me then, enroped, ensnared, entangled. Chittering teeth gnawed, sucking onto me as we fell together in a horrid embrace, as I stared close into those blind-seeing eyes, squid-grip tightening, cinching around my chest, fingers digging into my throat like a hangman's noose, constricting like an anaconda, tightening the clutch with each exhalation of its prey. Blood dripped. Flies buzzed. Willoughby's shattered face just leered above, poised, watching, waiting, grinning closer and closer. Ragged teeth and foul breath and bone white eyes. I was done for. In the slick mess, almost unconscious through deprivation, I knew I could not give in. I fought. Struggled. Kicked. Slipped a hand free, an arm! Screaming, thrusting up, enveloping my hand in a glove of his flesh, I squirmed it into that ragged shotgun-blown hole in his side. Gripping a fistful of his jellied squid sinew, pumping cold and slick in my trembling fist, I twisted. I tore. I pulled. And Willoughby … he fell.

I clambered upon him in his throes. Crimson he grinned still as his life drained free in an ever widening pool of inevitability. "Wilbur … Wilbur is still alive," he said. I leaned forward. "A gift…" he hissed. With dying breath upon his lips, he whispered to me where Wilbur was and how I could get there. I thought it at first some last act of contrition of a dying man; then I thought it a trick, a falsehood, only later realizing the harsh truth. '*His gift*' was not him sharing his secret with me. '*His gift*' was his act of sending us to that foul place. '*We*' were a gift to '*them*.'

We departed for it, nonetheless.

With difficulty and time and slow steady pressure, hauling our immense packs lodged full of ammo and implements of destruction, hacking through jungle vine and fording black bottomless rivers, Scarsdale and I found it. Finally. Upon the severed shores of a vestigial river bend it lay. An oxbow lake, where Willoughby had said it would. A pyramid rose above, the likes of which even Scarsdale had never heard, a mountain of skull and cracked bone. Refuse of ages gone to dust littered the grounds: moldering oxford shoes, a pair of bifocal glasses, some hapless policeman's shining tin badge … a child's doll. And there were older artifacts: a conquistador's rusted helm, twin cannon, thirty-two pounders each, lodged upright in the muck, yawning cyclopean toward the empty night.

Tattered, stumbling wraiths we were by now. But despite this, a grim elation carried us onward. So close. Like wild Indians we crept on hand and knee through the skittering filth.

We circumnavigated the skeletal mount, trying to ascertain the most likely whereabouts of prisoners. We found nothing, no one, only dread, only silence. Our meager hope faded with every moment. But once before, you dreamt of Wilbur somewhere deep beneath the earth. Brother, I put no stock in dreams, but you do and always have, and they had proved prophetic before. And thus, we uncovered a cave entrance within the skeletal mount, leading down. Into this claustrophobic fish-stinking fissure we slid, feet first, inching down, creeping, squeezing, contorting through cracks and beneath perilous stone, down, down, ever down into the bowels of black earth. Our electric torches had long since given in to jungle rot, and so we travelled on blind, our groping hands slithering along slick limestone walls until up ahead, my gun levelled, a green shimmer grew.

Within an endless limestone cavern, upon the shores of a subterranean lake, we found them. The tribe. I will not call them men. Some undoubtedly once were, somewhat akin to Willoughby; others were shorn completely of any ties to mankind in their plummeting degradation down the evolutionary rungs to fish, and frog, and thing of scale. Wilbur was correct, squid, an apt name. Some sort of depraved bacchanal, madness-cavorting, rioted on full bore, churning in the shallows as we approached, clandestine, huge green fires the source of the wavering light. It seemed. But no. The light came from the water. Rippling swirls of sea greens and glacier blues, waves of beautiful light and infinite dark, all in chaotic symphony undulated across silent stone, flickering like firelight. We crawled on past, daring no more than a glance.

Within a claustrophobic grotto, behind a rusted gate slapped across its entrance, we found Wilbur. He lay

The Brazil Business

amongst others, all broken, all used creatures, each one given to some element of degenerational change. Wilbur was no exception. Wasting no time, I stormed in through them, heaving Wilbur's skeletal frame up, dragging him free. Barely able to stand, barely conscious, he sputtered suddenly to life, his eyes full of a hideous vigor. "No!" His slurred cry echoed like across a canyon, reverberating on and on and on. He screamed — he wailed — he fought. A backhand across the face silenced him, breaking him from his stupor.

But the alarm had been raised. Captives bolted. Between us, Scarsdale and I dragged Wilbur across rock and stone as the first of the squids beset us. It snatched one of the fleeing captives first, dragging it squealing like a rabbit kicking into the glimmering shallows, its fingers cutting bleeding furrows in the sharp grit.

Then on like the rushing sea they came, charging, slithering, things of the deep, rolling boneless toward us in waves, breaking only upon hard-driven lead. Scarsdale dragged Wilbur on. I turned, striding backwards, a bulwark covering the retreat, blasting both barrels of my shotgun, slinging it behind, unslinging my Holland and Holland. Blasting again away. But they were behind us as well — Wilbur screamed, roaring in madness as twin horrors descended upon him, wrestling him to the ground, Scarsdale knocked aside. A melee of fist and nail and roped-sinew ensued, the twin squids getting the better of it.

Seven consecutive blasts ended it. Pious little Scarsdale stood there staring down at his own hands, your old .45 caliber clutched between them, barrel smoking, a look of despair upon his face that I shall never forget. Wilbur, though, back amongst the living, regained his feet and snatched the double-barrel from my shoulder, reloaded it, and brought it to bear, for on they came still. Behind the squids, slithering primordial from the foaming green, something pale and huge emerged, stirred from the depths. The very air seemed sucked from the cavern. Its many faceted eyes emerged, glistening eructations, glaring with inhuman passion as it snatched up the remaining captives in its many slithered embrace … and took them … invading them. The bioluminescent translucence of the thing was horror incarnate, and to witness those poor creatures writhing within…

Howling mad, Wilbur and I stood shoulder to shoulder, guns roaring, blazing away with a reckless abandon matched not even by the German machine gunners during those suicidal charges across no man's land. Till empty we fired, then thrusting our shotguns behind us to the prim, proper, pious Scarsdale, shells cascading as he scooped them up, fist-fucking them into breach faster than a cocaine-addled Ghurkha rifleman.

A mountain of carnage our fusillade wrought, poured on fierce, telling on the squids, but our ammo ran low then was gone. A moment later the squids had Wilbur, overpowering him, dragging him to the ground. I maintained my feet, slashing and slamming, hammering two-fisted with brass-knuckled trench knives. Severing tentacles, crushing skulls, hurling them back, back, back. But on they kept coming, wave after wave breaking over me, drowning me in tentacle and cold flesh. And it, it kept on coming, that pale hungry thing, its glistening pseudopods groping along the ground, palpating soft across the rock, oozing ever towards us.

Within Dr Scarsdale lay our salvation. A braver man there never was, and as Wilbur and I lay prone, pinned, crushed beneath that biting weight, shackled within the slick embrace of these eldritch horrors, Scarsdale tore suddenly from the shadows, past, his ever present crucifix clutched in one hand, a fistful of dynamite in the other, short fuse streaming behind, sparking, alive. Over the pack he clambered, fuse burning, fighting across the terrain of grasping flesh. And he fought free, running to greet the great pale thing. It snatched him up its roiling embrace, engulfing him bodily.

The explosion was deafening, the bodies upon us shielding against the blast.

Scrambling up, broken, beaten, I grabbed Wilbur, unconscious, slung his arm across my shoulder and mine about his waist and lifted him, dragging him up, dragging him out.

Behind us, the pale thing keened...

Upon a time, I once heard tell that the loveliest trick the devil ever played was convincing man that he did not exist. It was not. It was convincing man that God did.

And that, little brother, as they say, is the long and the short of it. I write this as I languish in prison, awaiting trial for the murder of Doctor Giles Willoughby. Irony, is it not? The warden says I need not worry, for there are certain things not to be brought to light, but he is a small man, and I refer not only to his stature. A firing squad stands outside this red brick sarcophagus, plying its trade, rifles firing from dawn till dusk. There are worse deaths.

I wish that I could be there for little Henry, for you, for you all, but it is out of my hands now. I hope only this letter somehow reaches you.

Farewell,

Edward

P.S. You should hear from Wilbur shortly, but if you do not, then not at all.

The Brazil Business

Postmarked from:

Danvers Asylum

450 Maple Street

Danvers, Massachusetts

Dear Gilbert,

The time is near. It is not much, but at least I can do for dear Henry that which I could not for my beloved Kate. I can be here when he passes. I can be here by his side and hold his hand throughout. It is a small thing, perhaps, but it is all I can do.

You told me reluctantly in a previous letter how Samuel, by accident, over a year past, referred to you as *'father.'* You were horrified, you had said. Horrified that in their minds you might supplant me. It struck a chord of sorrow within me at the time, a chord of wretched self-pity that laid me so low, so barren, so broke, but it was no accident. It was no error. It was the simple harsh truth gleaned from the mouths of babes, as they say. And it is now that very memory which guides me, bringing me, if not joy, then some modicum of strength, and dare I say it, hope. It draws me back from the brink where I have subsisted for so very long. My children will have lives. That drives me onward. A father. A mother.

A home. Perhaps, even normal lives. They have not seen me, nor have you, but I have seen you all here. That is not my wish, but it is my design. I have been gone so long and have changed so much. Your fears on that account were warranted, and as always, prophetic. It would be the utmost cruelty for me to appear to them after so long and in my present state. It would break them.

Sad it is that upon a quest whose ultimate goal was to prolong life there should be so much death. But life can be the worse of the two. I have seen it. I live it. A shoddy, shivering, desiccated existence. Did you know, brother, that I found it, found what I had first sought, deep within those caverns? Or perhaps it found me.? Nonetheless, it exists, eternal life. And although it was almost my doom, and is certainly my undoing, when the darkness falls still I yearn for it, beg for it, that prurient bliss, that nightmare kiss. Even now. That thing. It calls to me; it calls offering that which I sought, that which I crave. It took them within itself. They went willingly. They all went willingly, and still they exist. Their siren song I hear, pulling, wails of such pain, such … ecstasy. I understand. I envy. I want. I need. It would be so easy… Edward tore me from its cloying embrace like a babe from its womb, but only momentarily, for its pull is strong … it is steady … it is deep. I shall speak no more of it, for even the mere thought…

The Brazil Business

I must persevere.

I love you, dear brother. Ever were you my stalwart rock, doing that which I could not. I thank you for all those labors, those horrors you have endured, for I have learned, despite all I have gone through, that to remain as death takes its course and be able to do nothing but watch and offer ephemeral comfort is infinitely more difficult than seeking to circumvent it as I have done. I've walked in your shoes, here at the asylum, sitting by poor, dear Henry's side, night after night, reading him books, his favorite books. I don't know that he hears me.

Kate was cursed. Henry is cursed, and I? I am thrice-damned. It is we three who must pay the price, bear the brunt. In their sufferings, my wife and my child, there is no rhyme or reason, but perhaps this is enough. Perhaps it tips the scales back even.

I must stop writing this.

The time is now. It is not much, but at least I can do for dear Henry that which I could not for my beloved Kate. I can go with him when he passes. I can be here by his side and hold his hand throughout, and he mine. It is a small thing, perhaps, but it is all I can do.

Yours through eternity,

Wilbur

Kevin Wright

A Word from the Authors

Hello from Gary Bonn,

I live in Scotland, with my family and a cat that thinks he's an opera singer.

I also live in a fantasy land populated with everything from genetically-engineered aliens to mischievous pixies. I write when I'm not out in the hills, sinking in peat, and falling off my mountain-bike.

If you're looking for a short story to relax to — or be terrified by — do go to the links listed below at my website and WriterLot. There are lots of stories in many genres — and they're all free! Also, my two novels are listed below.

I hope you've enjoyed my work — or that you will. Do join me in fantasy land. See you soon.

Other Works by Gary Bonn:

The Evil And The Fear: Young Adult Supernatural Action Adventure: http://amzn.to/1sYE0Rr

Expect Civilian Casualties: Young Adult Paranormal Action Adventure: http://amzn.to/Y6tyi6

WriterLot link: http://writerlot.net/

Gary Bonn's website: http://garybonn.com/

* * * *

JAE ERWIN

JAE ERWIN writes, teaches yoga, and supports people through major life changes. She lives on the wild Pennine hills in the UK. She loves reading fiction — thrillers, crime and suspense — especially if there is a thread of the weird and mystical running through. Jae has a passion for the desert, tribal cultures and nomadic mysticism and has had one or two desert adventures of her own.

She has a degree and a Masters in psychology, has trained in Integral Psychotherapy and is fascinated with personality dynamics which can be healed with more holistic healing methods, combining both modern and ancient, such as mixing psychotherapy with shamanic practices and energy work.

Inspiration for her first novel, *Stillness Dancing*, came from a trip to Sinai and reading kidnapping accounts from the Middle East, most notably, *An Evil Cradling* by Brian

Keenan. JAE has three more novels in progress and has written many short stories, several of them published. A poem or six lurks in her dim and distant past.

Julie

Other works by JAE Erwin:

Stillness Dancing Amazon UK: http://amzn.to/1wLjhXU

Stillness Dancing Amazon US: http://amzn.to/1n2CE9i

WriterLot link: http://www.writerlot.net/JAE.htm

* * * *

Name: Patrick LeClerc a.k.a. Paracynic

Genus: Writicus Deadbeaticus

Habitat: Comfortable in any given hive of scum and villainy

Nest: Sturdy cardboard boxes, often under bridges, floored with nice, soft, empty liquor bottles

Traits: Never met a promotion he couldn't sabotage or a powerful ally he couldn't alienate. Will be steadfastly loyal to anyone who is in no position to do him a favor.

When not writing he is known to jockey ambulances, brew his own beer, dodge creditors, and fence. With swords, not stolen goods, which surprises those who know him well.

Other works by Patrick LeClerc:

Every Clime and Place: http://amzn.to/1viHzVe

Out of Nowhere: http://amzn.to/1v1epMe

Patrick LeClerc's website:

http://www.inkandbourbon.com/about.html

* * * *

Russell Jones

Russell Jones is a new writer with work that includes fantasy, the supernatural, and science fiction. He also tells other people's stories as a journalist working in Louisiana TV news, and loves crawfish boils almost as much as the mountains of Arkansas where he grew up. Russell is also working on his first novel and has two fiction serials running at Writerlot.net.

Other Works by Russell Jones:

WriterLot link: http://www.writerlot.net/RJ.htm

* * * *

William Sauer a.k.a Boopadoo

I am a former musician, former photographer, graphic designer by day, book designer and writer by night and weekend. I've scribbled down millions of words since childhood; the words just come, and who am I to try and stop them? Husband, brother to a legion of siblings, doggie daddy to mutts and strays. Often mistaken for a big, dumb gorilla until proven otherwise, which is how I like it. Then it's always a pleasant surprise when the truth is discovered: that boy can write, can't he? Especially when it's me doing the discovering.

Other Works by William Sauer:

WriterLot link: http://www.writerlot.net/Boopadoo.htm

* * * *

Kevin Wright

Kevin Wright studied writing at the University of Massachusetts in Lowell and fully utilized his bachelor's degree by seeking and attaining employment first as a produce clerk and later as an emergency medical technician and firefighter.

For decades now he has studied a variety of martial arts but steadfastly remains not-tough in any way shape or form. He just likes to pay money to get beat up, apparently.

Kevin Wright peaked intellectually in the seventh grade.

He enjoys reading a little bit of everything and writing sci fi, fantasy, and horror. He does none of it well. *Revelations*, his debut novel, is his second venture into the realm of novel writing. His first was nigh-unreadable. Kevin continues to write in his spare time and is currently working on another full length novel.

Other Works by Kevin Wright:

Revelations: http://amzn.to/1rbza7Q

WriterLot link: http://www.writerlot.net/kevinwright.htm

Dear Reader,

Thank you very much for your readership. I hope you enjoyed Dark Covenants. If you would, please take a moment to review Dark Covenants online at: http://amzn.to/1tmeUlH.

Thanks again,

Kevin Wright

www.ingramcontent.com/pod-product-compliance
Lightning Source LLC
Chambersburg PA
CBHW031950170626
46807CB00006B/2426